Jean-Baptiste Andrea was born in 1971 in Saint-Germain-en-Laye and grew up in Cannes. Formerly a director and screenwriter, he published his first novel, *Ma Reine*, in 2017. It won twelve literary prizes, including the Prix du Premier Roman and the Prix Femina des Lycéens.

Sam Taylor is an author and former correspondent for *The Observer*. His translations include Laurent Binet's *HHhH*, Leïla Slimani's *Lullaby* and Maylis de Kerangal's *The Heart*, for which he won the French-American Foundation Translation Prize.

Also by Jean-Baptiste Andrea:

A Hundred Million Years and a Day

DEVILS AND SAINTS

GALLIC

DEVILS AND SAINTS

Jean-Baptiste Andrea

Translated from the French by Sam Taylor

Gallic Books
London

A Gallic Book

First published in France as *Des diables et des saints*
Copyright © L'Iconoclaste, 2021
English translation copyright © Sam Taylor, 2022

First published in Great Britain in 2022 by
Gallic Books, 12 Eccleston Street, London, SW1W 9LT

ISBN 9781913547295

Typeset in Fournier MT by Gallic Books
Printed in the UK by CPI (CR0 4TD)

2 4 6 8 10 9 7 5 3 1

Adagio sostenuto

Si deve suonare tutto questo pezzo delicatissimamente e senza sordino

You know me. Just think, and you'll remember. The old man who plays those public pianos that you see in various transport hubs. On Thursdays I'm at Orly, and on Fridays at Charles-de-Gaulle. The rest of the week I play in train stations, other airports, anywhere I can find a piano. I can often be found at the Gare de Lyon because I live nearby. You have probably heard me more than once before.

One day, at last, you come closer. If you are a man, you won't say anything. You will pretend to tie your laces so that you can listen to me without it being obvious. If you are a woman, I will probably look a little startled. Because I am waiting for a woman. Don't worry, it's not you. I have been waiting for her for more than fifty years.

You have a thousand faces. I remember each of them, I forget nothing. You are that girl on pale mornings bouncing back and forth between the city and the suburbs. You are that man in a dark suit about whom I remember thinking: 'I bet he makes love with the zeal of a bureaucrat,' even if, obviously, this is none of my business – I am the first to acknowledge that women are a complicated matter. You are white, you are blue, red, green, you are all the colours of the rainbow. You wander around my pianos looking lost because I am not asking for money. Then you approach me. You all ask me the same question:

'What's a man like you doing in a place like this?'

What does that mean, I ask, 'a man like me'?

And you always answer in more or less the same way: 'A well-groomed man like you, even if you missed part of your left cheek when you shaved this morning. A well-dressed man like you, even if your tie is a bit old-fashioned. A man, basically, who can play the piano like you can. You play like a god – perhaps you play for Him? A talent like yours should not be wasted in train stations or airports. You play like those pianists who enchant audiences all over the world in the great concert halls. But here, you are only enchanting the wet tarmac and some rain-drenched hats.'

You're right, madam. Very perspicacious of you, sir. My concert venues have terrible acoustics and they smell of metal tracks and jet fuel. My Scalas and Carnegie Halls have names like Montparnasse, Roissy, Union Station, John F. Kennedy Airport. And there is a good reason for that. But it's a long story and I don't want to bore you.

You go on your way, most of you. Occasionally you do not give up. You offer me a large sum of money to play for your mother on her birthday, at a dinner party, a bar mitzvah, and you see me hesitate. You suggest introducing me to your husband, a senior manager at the Philharmonie de Paris. Or your uncle, who is a talent agent for musicians. Each time, I decline politely: thank you, truly, it was very kind of you to offer. I would make a very poor guest. The only places I like are wide-open spaces, with gusts of wind and slamming doors.

Yesterday you asked me: 'Will you be here tomorrow?'

Tomorrow is neither Thursday nor Friday, so yes, of course I'll be here.

A C sharp fades to silence between the departure of the 19:03 to Annecy and the arrival of the 19:04 from Béziers; please move away from the edge of the platform. Oh, you came back? I'll introduce myself, in that case. My name is Joe. It's short for Joseph, of course, but nobody has called me Joseph in a long time. Joseph is the name of a great musician, and the name of the Messiah's father.

You ask me to play again. You want to test me. To understand. Is there a trick to it? Today you tell me you want to hear Berg, or Brahms.

I'm sorry, but I play only Beethoven.

You find me a little bit annoying, I can tell. Forgive me. I have been this way for fifty years – it's too late to change my habits now.

'All right then, play the first movement of the "Moonlight Sonata",' you reply. 'Even if it is very … classic.'

You almost said 'banal', and you would not be the first. You glance at your watch – you don't want to miss that dinner in town, your friends or your colleagues are expecting you, the appetisers are ready. Hands raised, I wait for the rhythm. With a dying gasp, a TGV locomotive comes to a halt on Platform L: an electric whale that has swum all the way from Nice at three hundred kilometres per hour. Inside, the bodies stretch then rush out towards sleep, alcohol, boredom, heart attacks, who knows what else. It's all there, hopes and abandonments. You don't hear it.

I touch the keyboard. The furious arpeggio, the chords, *presto agitato*. The third movement, not the one you asked for; I don't like anything predictable. Your lips retract. Your pupils change size, a drug addict breathing freely again after an injection of adrenaline. When it ends you are silent for a long time.

You have been hit full in the face by a tornado, like thousands of others before you. It lifted you up, wrung you out and dropped you back in the same spot. You can't quite believe you are still alive. Never will you use the word 'banal' again. I know what you're feeling. One cannot hear a genius become deaf without a certain emotion.

You say: 'A musician of your calibre … You should be given the Légion d'honneur, people should be speechless in your presence. But everyone just ignores you. Haven't you ever thought of performing?'

Performing? That's all I do.

Your smile twitches with impatience, exposing your teeth.

'I mean performing on stage. You wouldn't be the first musician with a late-flowering career. Honestly, you're still quite young.'

Thank you, madam, thank you, sir. But I have to stay here. I don't want to miss the last train. The last plane. You can keep your Légions d'honneur, your medals, those ornaments that sting then numb your heart.

'You could make a lot of money, Joseph. Buy your own piano.'

It's Joe, not Joseph. I don't need money. I have all the pianos I want. And I am not young – I'm sixty-nine years old. I can tell from the look in your eyes that you're about to protest. Let me stop you there; this is not a question of vanity. What I'm telling you is true. I have not been young for a long, long time. In fact, I remember the precise hour when I stopped being young.

Let's go and sit at that terrace over there. The coffee isn't good, but the seats are comfortable. I think, this time, that I am going to have to explain it all to you.

It all started when I became ill. An incurable disease. Don't panic, it's not contagious. It struck me down on 2 May 1969. I didn't do anything to bring it about. Anyone who catches it would tell you the same thing.

My infirmity is not mentioned in any medical encyclopaedia. It should be.

My father said that a man cannot live without two essential items: a good mattress and a good pair of shoes. He sold both these items. Not together, obviously. The mattress factory he inherited from his mother, a good Englishwoman in every respect ... well, in almost every respect, because she became pregnant during her holidays in France just before the war and ended up settling here. The shoes came later. When my father, an elegant man, learned that his shoemaker was about to go bankrupt, he bought the business from him.

My father excelled at everything. Music. Gardening. Sport. He could have been a doctor, an architect. He could have been a priest, or a rabbi, but he didn't believe in God and he wasn't Jewish. Not completely, anyway: his mother wasn't Jewish, so he wasn't either, and I am even less so. According to my father, this was no bad thing. His suppliers, good Catholics all, reproached him as it was for driving too hard a bargain. He did not want to be accused, on top of that, of the attempted murder of their Saviour, particularly with the Americans offering ever tougher competition. When my mother suggested that it might be an idea to tell me about that part of my history, my quarter-Jewishness, he grew angry. We never spoke of the matter again.

My parents raised me like a project, with the energy of dictators. They loved me like a five-year plan. But they loved me. I was *their* five-year plan. Only my unbearable sister escaped their tyranny, because she was three. At just over a thousand days old, Inès believed there was nothing she wasn't allowed to do. She went through my things, touched my vinyl records. If I shouted at her, she would cry and I would be the one who was punished. Unbearable.

A few days before my illness, completely unaware that we were all incubating the disease, my father took me to his office.

'I just talked to Rothenberg. He told me that you have not been doing well recently. That you are becoming lazy. He says, if this continues, you will not be admitted into the next year at the conservatory. He believes you are wasting your talent. What do you have to say for yourself?'

There was an obvious explanation: I had been smoking vine leaves with my best friend Henri in the woods behind his parents' manor house instead of practising my scales.

'I don't know. It's a mystery to me. I work hard.'

'Not hard enough, apparently. Your mother, your sister and I will go to Rome without you this weekend. You should use the time alone to think about what you want to do with your life.'

I begged my father. I begged my mother, who refused to listen. She also gave me some history homework (my mother was an eminent history teacher). I speak about her today with tenderness, because of what happened afterwards. The years of black rain that chilled me to the bone. But that day, I felt no tenderness at all. I hated my parents.

We lived in the Paris region. I was about to turn sixteen and I had never wanted for anything. My life smelled of leather and orchids, of Dior perfumes, and it was safely circumscribed by the brick wall around our property. When night fell I would dream of running away, changing the world. Yelling orders in Spanish at my faithful guerrilla fighters, a beret on my head and a cigar between my lips. But first I had to learn Spanish. So ... one day. Later. In the meantime, my revolutionary ambitions died each morning I was given breakfast in bed. I was a normal boy, in other words. A typical bourgeois teenager, an affable idiot.

Even so, I don't think I did anything to deserve that disease.

'The rhythm!' Rothenberg shouted at me. 'The rhythm!' Old

Rothenberg taught me piano. His skin was like crumpled paper, his face, neck and hands a Braille text of dizzyingly complex wrinkles.

But when he played.

When he played, the Three Wise Men set off on their way. Exotic princesses in distant lands grew languid in their palaces of sand. Even Madame Rothenberg, a withered shadow who smelled of mothballs, became once again the southern queen who had seduced him, sixty years before, under a flowering walnut tree.

Rothenberg taught nothing but Beethoven. In a far-flung past of which he spoke only rarely, the great German composer — whom he called by his first name — had saved his life. Rothenberg had played his thirty-two sonatas day after day, without an instrument. Fingers in the air, feet in the dust of Poland, he had played to stop himself going mad.

When I asked him if we could study something else, he lost his temper.

'You are *already* studying something else, you imbecile! In Ludwig's music, there is everything. Before and after. There is Bach, there is Schubert. There is Gabrieli, Mozart, Bruckner. It wouldn't be that much of a stretch to say there is Varèse too. What more do you want?'

That week — the week I fell sick, the week when he called my father — I had driven him to despair. I insulted the rhythm, and Rothenberg, in agony, tore out his hair. Or, at least, what little remained of it in the ginger crown that encircled the speckled skin of his scalp. His head made me think of a leopard in flames.

'In the Andante of Sonata no. 15, the rhythm is essential. You see what it's called?'

I leaned forward to read the score.

'Um, "Pastoral".'

'What's it about?'

'Woods?' I shrugged. 'Streams?'

'*Schmegegge!* Woods, streams ... what rubbish! You hear this beat with the left hand? That's a guy stepping over your woods. He's climbed on the shoulders of Bach to see over the trees. And you, you play it like some *schmock* who's fallen asleep in the grass after eating too much food. Like a drunkard in search of a woman in the Bois de Boulogne! Shift up, for God's sake, I'll show you.'

'Calm down, Alon,' said Madame Rothenberg from the kitchen. 'Don't forget what the doctor told you.'

He became one with the piano without even sitting down. And I saw things that I would understand only later. I saw giants dancing. I saw an eagle swoop down and weave a blue hem on the surface of a lake. When he stopped playing, I started to yell because I had been afraid. Afraid of being crushed. Afraid of being swept away.

'What's the point? I'll never be able to play like that! I'll never be able to play like you!'

Rothenberg closed the piano lid and covered it with a macramé doily before turning slowly to face me. I thought he was going to slap me, but he gently touched his paper hand to my cheek.

'No, you will never play like me, my boy. But if you keep on the way you are going, something worse will happen. You will never play like you.'

I left, high on the first rage of adolescence, my fists full of thunderbolts ready to be thrown at happiness.

Unaware that I would never see Alon Rothenberg again.

If I had stayed at home, nothing would have happened. But, almost as soon as my parents left for their stupid weekend in Rome, almost as soon as their taxi disappeared at the end of the avenue, I ran to Henri's house.

Henri Fournier was my best friend – we had made an oath. The Fourniers were rich, even richer than us. He too had an unbearable sister, only his was older, which presented certain advantages when she took a shower without remembering to close the door. His father had made his fortune in screws – wood screws, sheet-metal screws, self-drilling screws, lag screws – screws of all types which he imported from Asia. Henri and I often listened to music, the kind of music that our parents described as 'degenerate'. That day, it was a brand-new 33 rpm that he had brought back the previous night from Paris: the Rolling Stones. The record-shop owner had sworn to Henri that they were as degenerate as could be, and he was not wrong. We bounced on his bed, shaking our imaginary long hair.

We turned the record over. The stylus descended. Static, tribal drums, wild yelps and shrieks, women's laughter, piano. I stopped jumping. Rothenberg was right. The rhythm. These guys had found it. A rhythm to lead us to the end of the world. To drown us in the sea, a whole generation, if they felt like it. The sound of raised voices in the entrance hall. *Jump!* yelled Henri. *Jump higher!* I was paralysed. *Woo-woo!* Those savages were calling their god now. *Woo-woo!* And still I could hear raised voices in the entrance hall.

'Henri, there's someone shouting downstairs.'

Henri lifted up the arm of the record player. His father came hurtling into the entrance hall at the same moment we did. In the doorway, Madame Fournier was spluttering at a man half invisible inside a jacket that was too large for him, carrying a drawing under his arm.

'What on earth is this racket?' Monsieur Fournier demanded. 'Can't a man read his newspaper in peace in this house?'

'I am part of the Foyer Sacré-Cœur,' the visitor recited. 'A charitable association that helps ex-prisoners reintegrate into society. I would like to show you some paintings. Well, just one in fact – the only one I have left – and then my day is over. You can give as much or as little as you like.'

'How did you get in?'

'That's what I asked him!' shouted his wife. 'He says he pushed open the gate.'

'The gate is locked. You jumped over the wall, didn't you?'

The man shrugged. 'No, I pushed open the gate. Please, just five minutes. Take a look at what we do, give as much as you like. If you don't like the painting, you don't have to give anything. Or just a few coins, to help us out.'

'Oh yes? I'll help you out, just you see. Wait there.'

Fournier disappeared and came back less than thirty seconds later with a rifle. He had a collection of weapons that he never used. Once, when Henri and I had been left alone in the house, we had loaded one of those guns. Henri had wanted to kill the neighbours' big ginger cat. I had forced him to choose between his friendship with me and the ginger cat, and in the end we had killed some bottles instead. I wasn't especially fond of that cat, but still, there were limits.

The man took a step back when he saw the gun. When Fournier loaded a cartridge and fired a warning shot into the air, he ran for his life. We saw him disappear towards the bottom of the garden and jump over the wall. Because, of course, the gate was locked. Henri's mother bent down to pick up the folder that the man had dropped. Inside was one single gouache, showing a deformed-looking Christ, his head on his shoulder amid a fog of thorns. There was a baleful, twisted look to everything in the painting – the mouth, the eyes, the shoulders, the cross – all of it as wrong as the original act of crucifixion. Even the letters ECCE HOMO were misshapen under the wash of gouache.

'Was it painted by a four-year-old or what?' Fournier sniggered. 'Seriously, though, look at it! And what's all this homo stuff? Is it a charity for queers?'

He burst out laughing. His wife copied him, and then Henri did the same. They were almost weeping with hilarity. I looked at the painting too and, since it was apparently the done thing, started laughing in turn, even louder than the others.

If I had just stayed at home, nothing would have happened. The disease would have passed through me without harm. It would have moved on to strike down some other moron, a few streets away; there was no shortage of stupid people in our neighbourhood. But no, I had to go out. I had to *laugh*. Like that shoemaker, Ahasverus, who – according to legend – taunted Jesus on his way to the cross and was afterwards condemned to wander the earth until the Second Coming.

One cannot laugh with impunity at a man's misfortune.

The next day – the day of my parents' return – I awoke with a strange feeling. The first mysterious symptom. I stood naked in front of my mirror. Tongue: normal. Eyes: bright. No physical sign of my malaise. The only things that were wrong with me were the things that were always wrong: my moustache, which still obstinately refused to grow, and – even more depressingly – my puny physique. And yet I worked out every morning, following the exercises in a callisthenics training manual that I had ordered by post. The advertisement, lavishly illustrated, had promised to transform me, in less than ninety days – satisfaction guaranteed or my money back – into a colossus capable of teaching a lesson to any boorish male bothering a woman on a beach. In the last drawing, the woman appeared very, very grateful.

After my physical exercises, I began practising the piano. I tried to find that rhythm I had heard the day before, from the Stones song. Almost everyone I knew thought I played beautifully. I was often asked to perform at the school's end-of-year party, and all the girls would look at me. But none of these people had heard old Rothenberg. When *his* fingers touched the keyboard, they spoke of the sweetness of the Rhine one spring evening, nights in Vienna and Heiligenstadt, the blue of fireworks, the black of despair, the gathering silence, everything that Ludwig had expressed to him. The only thing my fingers communicated, to anyone willing to listen, was my utter mediocrity.

Around five o'clock, Monsieur Albert rang the doorbell. My father's secretary had offered to pick my parents up from Le Bourget Airport and he had suggested that I go with him. We arrived in time to stand by the side of the runway, in the hot wind, and watch as the Sud-Aviation Caravelle SE 210 descended from the sky. Like all boys my age, I was mad about aeroplanes. I reeled off its vital statistics: 'Rolls-Royce Avon engines; compression ratio of 7.45 to 1; mass flow of 68 kilograms per second …' Monsieur Albert nodded. He had no idea what I was talking about. Although, to be honest, neither did I. The aeroplane made its approach.

I had a sudden feeling of unease. Inexplicable. I swear I heard the second movement of Sonata no. 8. I heard it the way Ludwig himself must have played it, with that *rhythm*, as beautiful as the Caravelle in the blazing sunset, sinking softly into a dream of rivets. The music bent me over the barrier, covered in sweat. And the Caravelle, as it softly landed, broke in two, just like that, for no reason whatsoever, fell apart before our very eyes, the front part going one way, the back half the other, before transforming into an immense and perfectly round ball of fire. I can still feel that perfect roundness even now, when I wake, my hands cupped to hold it in, to stop it escaping, because I know that deep within the ball, at that exact moment, my parents and my unbearable sister are still alive, and that whatever I do I must not let go of it.

My youth ended at 6:14 p.m. on 2 May 1969, in a polka of flames and crosswinds. 'The abnormally elevated angle of incidence, combined with the underestimated speed and the presence of a strong crosswind, led the aircraft to stall.' I learned the report's conclusions by heart; all I had to do to put an end to the questions was recite these words in a serious voice. It worked every time, except with the psychologist I was forced to see three times, who appeared interested in the details.

'Fournier residence. Hello?'

My parents' death taught me one thing: I had no one else in the world. My mother was an only child. And while my father was officially only half Jewish, his family had been deemed sufficiently Jewish for the good bureaucrats of Vichy. At the time, being half anything was frowned upon, and my father had only survived because a neighbour who was fully Aryan, beyond all suspicion, had agreed to hide him.

'Madame Fournier? It's Joe. Joseph.'

Painless. That was the first thing they said, the experts and everyone else. Your parents and your sister did not feel a thing.

'Hello, Madame Fournier? Are you there?'

'Yes. Hello, Joseph. Sorry, Henri has gone out.'

The experts also told me: it's not your fault. Which was all the proof I needed that they were liars.

'Gone out? But you told me to call today. When will he be there?'

'I don't know. You should probably just wait for him to call you back.'

Henri. My best friend.

'But they keep moving me around. Apart from the first week, when I stayed in the same centre and he forgot to call me back.'

We had sworn an oath.

'Yes. Well … All right. Goodbye then, Joseph.'

That was it, at that precise moment. Not when the aeroplane crashed. Not when my parents and Inès were vaporised, hand in hand − I hoped that they were holding hands. Not when I slept, that first night, among strangers. It was not until Madame Fournier hung up on me that I understood. I was sick. Of all the prophets' curses, of all the pestilences that ravage the earth, I had been struck down by the worst. I had been *orphaned*, in the same way that others catch leprosy, tuberculosis, plague. An incurable condition. To protect the healthy from my exhalations of pain and misery, I had to be kept apart from them. A simple prophylactic measure, in case it was contagious.

For two months I was shunted around between orphanages and foster families. I quickly familiarised myself with the hierarchy, invisible to most mortals, of the great nation of the lonely. First there were real orphans, the angels, whose parents were dead, deceased, pushing up daisies. And then the imitations: the children of drug addicts, abusers or alcoholics, whose parents were alive but incapable of bringing them up.

But we angels were not all equal. At the summit, the aristocracy of orphans, the crème de la crème, were the orphans of police officers. They had their own centres, which were spoken of in awed tones: whispered descriptions of table football tournaments, rooms containing only four beds. One notch below came the orphans of the wealthy. My parents were well-off, but in these situations the nature of the wealth was important. Old money was the best kind, the type passed down from generation to generation. More recent fortunes were tolerated if your parents had worked for the good of the nation. The children of arms dealers or senior government officials were second in rank only to the children of police officers.

And then there were the rest. Me. Since my family's wealth had been founded on shoes and mattresses, I was not worth much, even if my father had several times boasted of this or that minister's fondness for his tasselled moccasins, or another's love of the bounciness of his beds. I was a nobody, part of the great mass of estate-agent orphans, electrician orphans, the orphans of dawn wakings and frozen bank accounts, the orphans of debts or money considered dirty because it is not the blue of aristocratic blood or cannon barrels.

This is probably why I was sent there. Unless it was simply a mistake. Or an act of laziness. I never knew, and ultimately it matters little: the result was the same. I was sent to a place you have never heard of, because it is not on earth. I was sent to a place you will never hear about. It closed long ago.

An orphanage that went by the name of Les Confins. It has closed, but for some of us it remains an open wound.

The time matters. And so does the weather. We took the train from Paris to Toulouse, accompanied by a social worker, a bald man who smelled of cauliflower, with rings of sweat under his arms. Then we caught a bus, which broke down and did not arrive in Tarbes until midnight. There, Cauliflower Man handed us over to two gendarmes whose task it was to transport us to Les Confins.

I was travelling with a boy I didn't know. He was slightly older than me – maybe sixteen. Almost six feet tall and very thin, he had bushy hair and the ghost of a moustache, an admirably black collection of soft hairs. He was no mute, but I heard him say only two words in his life, both of them much later. When the gendarmes saw him, they made that international sign for someone who is not all there: the index finger drilling into the temple. He was dragging along an imitation-leather suitcase that the policemen were not able to take from him because he started moaning as soon as they tried. The suitcase took up all the space in the back seat of the car. A cuddly donkey was tied to it. The poor animal was not in the best of health: red tongue lolling from its mouth, foam innards pouring from a wound in its belly. Yet it clung to life, and Momo clung to it.

That was my travelling companion's name. I could see it scribbled on a label attached to the suitcase handle. Just that one name: Momo. On the back of the label were the words 'Intercontinental Hotel, Oran'. Momo looked exactly like a kid who used to live at the end of my street, the only *pied-noir* family in the neighbourhood. Happy or sad, they were always noisy, and just trashy enough for me to find them attractive. Madame Fournier accused them of bringing down property prices in the area.

The gendarmes were kind. Just before Lourdes they stopped at a roadside restaurant that never closed and bought us some chips. Even today, I can't see a gendarme without feeling an urge to eat chips, and then to hug him. When we set off again, the sky came alive with a storm of apocalyptic proportions. A biblical wrath, perhaps directed at me. We drove very slowly. The gendarmes discussed whether they should return the way they'd come or keep going. In the end, their chief – on the police radio – left them no choice: he did not want to get lumbered with two teenage boys. I stayed silent. Momo showed me a worn label that was tied to his donkey, not far from the wound in its belly. I read the faded letters: *Asinus*. The cuddly toy smelled of clinging sadness, of cargo holds and Saturdays that would never again be spent at the seaside.

'It's temporary,' a bearded man in an orange office had told me, just before our departure. 'You'll only be staying there while they find you a family. It won't take long, you'll see.'

The night boiled above us. It surged over mountains, poured through valleys. Now and then a flash of lightning would reveal the silver landscape. The rough black sides of a gorge. The slope of a forest. We kept driving. Momo smiled constantly: he could see something funny, something that remained invisible to the rest of us. Occasionally our eyes would meet, and then he would nod at me as if to say: *Just wait a bit longer, after this hill, after the fever, after the storm, you'll see, you'll understand, it's really very funny*. I am sixty-nine years old and I am still waiting, but perhaps I still have a few more hills left to climb.

The car came to a halt – a small landslide had blocked the road. One of the gendarmes got out, grumbling as he shoved the rocks out of the way. The other one turned on the radio.

The twenty-first of July 1969. I found out later, like everyone else, that it was 2:56 a.m., Greenwich Mean Time. A blizzard of static. Then an American voice, which I understood because my father spoke English fluently. It was Neil Armstrong.

'The surface is fine and powdery,' he said, and the radio presenter translated this into French.

Apollo 11, transmitted live all over the planet. I had studied the flight plan, I had even talked about it with Rothenberg. My father had promised me I would be able to stay up all night for this special event. On that night when we would, through the power of the nozzle and the afterburner, push back the frontier of darkness.

'Sir, can you turn it up?'

'Warrant officer, not sir,' the gendarme corrected me.

But he did it anyway; he was just as interested as I was. His colleague had come back in a bad mood, and now he was bent over the steering wheel, trying to keep us away from the edge of the road. Torrents drumming the windscreen, Moses floating past in a basket. What did he care about the moon?

'I'm gonna step off the ladder now.' I clung to that American voice. Silence, crackling. 'That's one small step for man' – Neil Armstrong paused for thought, or pretended to, given that his speech had been prepared beforehand – 'one giant leap for mankind.'

The driver turned off the radio.

'No!'

I had yelled, and now they were all staring at me strangely. Even Momo, who had been startled awake.

'We're here,' said the driver. 'Everybody out.'

We were soaked instantly. Far ahead of us, a door in the rain. No building visible around it, just a pale rectangle in a world of rain. Momo ran, protecting his donkey. Eventually the gendarmes realised that I wasn't with them. The warrant officer returned, water dripping from his furious face, ankle-deep in a magma of mud.

'Fucking move! What the hell are you doing, just standing there in the rain like an idiot?'

I could not tell him what I was doing there, standing in the rain like an idiot. I could not explain to him that it was taking me all my strength to stop myself yelling at the sky, beyond the storm, to prevent myself shouting at the top of my voice to ask Armstrong if he might, by any chance, in one of those craters, have seen my parents and my unbearable sister.

We were led through the bowels of the building by a lumbering man in his early fifties, a man with no neck and eyes too far apart. Inside, it smelled of lessons learned and prayers never granted. Ahead of me, Asinus bounced up and down on Momo's suitcase. The donkey's rancid stench stung the back of my throat, mingled with our guide's odour of sweat and tobacco. The corridor started to spin around me and I almost threw up my chips on the floor. The guide lit our way with a sort of luminous key fob, a ridiculous gadget that gave off a vaguely phosphorescent glow. The power was out.

He ushered us into a vast dormitory that resembled a crypt, divided in two by a velvet curtain. Dozens of beds were lined up there like tombs, each with its own recumbent statue. The statues were snoring.

'You here,' the man told Momo. 'And you there. I don't want to hear a sound.'

Momo lay down without taking off his shoes. His feet stuck out at the end of the bed.

'What are you waiting for?' the man asked me. 'The great flood? It's already here. So, lie down. Or you and I aren't going to be friends.'

The phosphorescence dimmed, his footsteps faded. I

remember it vividly, that night, the night of my arrival at Les Confins. I remember the noise that would be the background of my life for a year. A distant, muffled percussion, a strange kind of supersonic boom that hollowed my chest every thirty minutes and gave the impression that there was not enough air to breathe. That something had burst the atmosphere, deflated the world like a popped balloon. I held my breath. Then everything became normal again.

I remember turning to look at the bed next to mine. Empty. Or, at least, there was nobody on top of it. A second later, I saw a ginger boy lying *under* it, in the darkness, a kid my age with a long amphora-shaped face. He put a finger to his lips – *shhh* – then fell back asleep.

Un pas de géant pour l'humanité.

It sounds good, doesn't it, a giant leap for mankind? A few days later, Neil Armstrong, Buzz Aldrin and the third man whose name the world has forgotten – who would be forever after remembered simply as 'the third man' – returned as conquering heroes. Confetti rained down. Tubas roared, women fainted. Everybody talked about their American smiles, their white teeth, their heroic faces grinning from the back seats of convertibles long enough to lie down in, or to be killed in. Nobody talked about me.

And yet I deserve my share of the glory. I went to the moon too, that day: 21 July 1969. I swear I did. I went to the moon, and beyond, and I came back. Nobody knows it though. Nobody cares.

The humanity of small steps ... It doesn't have the same ring.

These days, you will have to ask for directions. At the local bar, for example, if it still exists. They will point out the road at the edge of the village, the last village in this Pyrenean valley. You will pass a few looming, indifferent houses and you will see that the road does indeed continue. This place must be frightening, you will think, on a dark and stormy night. Better not come up here when it's raining, when you're fifteen years old, when you have no parents.

If you are curious, if you are not there merely by chance, you will perhaps remark: *All the same, you must have known, when the kids came down to the village at Christmas or Bastille Day. Surely it was impossible not to notice it, the misery?* The villagers, if they remember at all, if any of them are still alive to remember that period, will reply that no, they didn't notice anything at all, the kids seemed happy to be in the village, they even bought a few things with their savings, but anyway all that is in the past, why are you asking so many questions?

You will follow the road, about ten kilometres long. You will stop at a sign, on which you can still read, despite the acid rain and the bullet holes, the inscription *Departmental Directorate of San ...* the letters one by one being eaten by rust. Then the words *Les Confins*, intact. The rust must have taken one taste and spat them out.

Beyond the sign, the road has not been maintained. You can't drive on it. You will have to walk to the former priory, which used to be called Saint-Michel-de-Geu. When you see it, you will wonder how they managed to build it there, at the bottom of that valley. Everything converges on a rock face one hundred metres high: the wind, the road, the country itself, because beyond that rock face is Spain. You will admire the ingenuity required to excavate a space big enough for that old building, here, in the mountains, at the end of the eighteenth century. If you have any taste, you will be less admiring of the building added in 1959 on one of the sides, where the children took classes.

You will also wonder what they were so ashamed of, the people who raised these walls. Nobody builds something this dark, this harsh, without a good reason. It was all because of a naked man in a garden and an apple, they will explain. If it hadn't been for that man and that apple, nothing would have happened. But there was a naked girl there too, and who can resist a naked girl? Hence the high windows, powerless to stop the wind. Hence the sharp slates, the infinite echoes, the church that is freezing cold in spring, summer, autumn, winter, freezing cold from evening until morning.

Beside the old priory, a few blunted terraces attempt to tame the steep slope. The old vegetable garden is still discernible. Far below, the last terrace runs alongside a disused railway line that vanishes into the undergrowth. If you cleared out the blackthorns, the brambles, the broom – no easy task, admittedly – you would discover a derelict tunnel. A masterpiece of civil engineering, five kilometres stolen from the mountain between France and Aragon.

Perhaps you will venture into the main building, ignoring the sign that reads *Danger: asbestos*. You won't find anything. Or nothing more than a single mimeographed sheet of paper, pinned beneath a broken window near the front door. Illegible, except for a few words: '05:45 … team games … Holy Word … Vercors'.

The place is quiet, almost beautiful when the sun shines. What strikes you is the silence. A silence of prayers and of corridors that never lead to the same place twice. I don't know why you have come here, if not to bang your head against the granite. In the end, you will go back the way you came, your questions – if you had any – unanswered.

It's all in the name. *Les Confins*: the outer reaches, the very edges. Beyond this place, there is nothing at all.

05:45 – reveille
06:00 – ablutions
06:30 – lauds (morning service)
07:00 – breakfast
08:00–11:00 – classes
11:00 – break (choice of activities: quiet team games, reading, prayers)
12:00–13:00 – lunch
13:00–16:00 – personal time (choice of activities: study, prayer, correspondence, nap time for younger children)
17:00–19:00 – collective chores
19:00 – dinner and reading of the Holy Word
20:00 – thanksgiving
20:30 – curfew

• *During holidays, classes are replaced with outside educational activities, weather permitting. The schedule will be displayed on the opposite wall.*

• *Any student who wishes to go to the DDASS activity centre in Vercors for the summer holidays is invited to make a request at the beginning of the year, since places are limited.*

• *No running inside the building. No one may leave without authorisation and adult supervision. More generally, no action or behaviour likely to stain the reputation of Les Confins will be tolerated. Suitable clothing must be worn in all circumstances. All breaches of the rules will be punished.*

The management of Les Confins, the Ministry of Education and the diocese wish you a very holy academic year 1969–1970.

Momo and I had not exchanged a word since we first met. I spoke to him for the first time that morning, in the orphanage courtyard.

'Fuck off!'

I had barely slept. Woken at dawn by a whistle blast, I had imitated the others, standing near the bed while the man who had greeted us – known to the students as Toad – walked along the rows of beds as if searching for something. There was a white enamel plaque bearing a number screwed to the wooden frame of each bed. I was number 54. My suitcase had disappeared, as had Momo's. The only thing they had left him was his donkey.

'Everything you need is in there,' Toad had told us, pointing to a trunk at the foot of our beds. 'Make it last.'

Clearly he didn't know that I would not be there for long, that my stay was only *temporary*. A second whistle blast and we raced to the bathroom. Only the first comers got hot water. There were big yellow soap bars, gritty to the touch, that smelled of lemons and feet. Poor people's soap – disgusting. Tepid water splashed on the face. Like the others, I was wearing a white shirt and a pair of ridiculous shorts I had found in my trunk, plus the shoes that went with them. If I'd turned up at my old school dressed like this, I would have been beaten to a pulp.

'Where did they get these clothes?' I asked, smirking. 'The nineteenth century?'

Silence. Nobody had spoken a word to me that morning. Nobody spoke at all in fact. At breakfast we had chocolate soup with bread and a bowl of coffee, even the little ones. There were about forty of us altogether, aged between five and seventeen.

Another whistle blast. Time to leave the refectory. Momo

followed me, accompanied by Asinus. *Peeeep.* 'Sing a new song to the Lord,' the boys sang, and I moved my lips silently in time. 'For He has performed wonders ...' The group had split in two now, and I was with the older ones. An affable nun, Sister Hélène, announced in a gentle voice:

'I am replacing our good father for his French class.'

I was not prepared for the test we had to take. Momo spent the whole hour staring at the paper and grinning, not writing a thing. We were taken into the old chapterhouse with its vaulted ceiling. The room was enormous and the plastered walls had eczema. Thirty desks stood crookedly inside it, as if there had just been an earthquake. It was permanently freezing. A monstrous fireplace sucked up all the warmth in summer and spat out snow in winter.

I only found out why I was so unpopular at break time. A tall boy came over, hands in his pockets. He looked at Momo, who had been following me around all morning with his stinky donkey.

'Is he your brother?'

'No, I don't know him.'

'Is he a mong or what? Why does he keep smiling like that?'

Momo smiled.

I shrugged. 'Yeah, he's a mong,' I replied in the same tone.

'Hey lads, look. The mong's got stains on his shoes. Let's shine 'em.'

The boy hawked up a mouthful of thick saliva and spat it on Momo's shoes. His acolytes copied him. Momo turned to me, his eyes full of noise and questions that never came out, trapped behind his lips. Since the others seemed to be waiting for something, I spat on his shoes too. And just to make sure those boys understood that I was one of them, I leaned towards Momo and said:

'Fuck off.'

I knew it wasn't Momo's fault that he had lived there, in that jasmine-scented, faraway land where girls fell for his ochre eyes. It wasn't his fault that he'd had to leave suddenly, without having a chance to say goodbye to his friends. Hurry, hurry, we've got to go, leave the dough there, someone else will bake it, come on, hurry up, pack your suitcase, leave behind the house and your memories, and only later, too late, on the boat to Marseille, would they realise that, in their haste, they had forgotten Momo's head. He himself – the little *pied-noir* who would dive for sea urchins – had not asked for any of this.

He didn't move, so I said it again.

'Go on, fuck off!'

Momo fell to the floor, his body stiff and bent at the waist. I had never seen an epileptic seizure before. Toad, who was watching us from a corner of the courtyard, must have seen plenty: he leapt up, ran to Momo, picked up his body like a sack of potatoes and carried him inside.

The seizure had wiped the smile off Momo's face. But it didn't stop him holding on tight to Asinus. Even when Toad threw him over his shoulder, Momo continued to cling with all his strength to its kingdom of fur.

'Have you seen *Mary Poppins*?'

The boy tugging at my sleeve could not have been older than eight or nine. A little kid, but beggars can't be choosers. We went round and round the courtyard, in small groups or alone, forty-three children who cast no shadow. Some of them were playing a chaotic game of football. I hadn't been invited to join their stupid team but maybe that was for the best. If I broke a hand or an arm, I could kiss goodbye to a career in music.

'Have you seen *Mary Poppins*?' the kid asked again.

He had a funny face, like that of a shrunken adult stuck between ears like the handles of a trophy. A fading shiner around his left eye. Massive gaps between his front teeth.

'*Mary Poppins*? No.'

'Pfft,' he replied.

'Hey, hang on! What's your name?'

His head came up to my navel, but I swear he looked me up and down before deigning to tell me what he was called.

'Souzix.'

He joined a small group of older kids: the boy who slept under his bed and two others – one fat, the other skinny. All three of them were the same age as me. I expected them to shove the little kid away, to make fun of this shrimp, this nobody who was trying to enter their adolescent circle, where faint moustaches and zits were marks of superiority. But they welcomed him as if he were one of them, leaning down to listen to him, glancing over in my direction. Then they all burst out laughing.

When I tried to join them, they turned away.

The noise had not stopped. The one I'd heard when I first arrived: that supersonic boom. It kept happening, every thirty minutes. I was the only one who jumped each time.

At 7 p.m. there was another whistle blast: time for my first dinner at Les Confins. A slice of toast covered with melted bone marrow and coarse salt. Everyone looked happy. For them, this was haute cuisine. I could never eat anything so fatty. In a corner of the refectory, a very small boy was haltingly reading out a passage of Scripture while the others chewed and whispered. Suddenly a door creaked and the atmosphere changed. The small boy stood up straight, he spoke in a louder, firmer voice. Heads were lowered over plates. Cutlery was placed on the table.

A distant *boom*.

That was when I saw him for the first time. He had a strong jaw, closely shaved. No trace of grey hair at his temples. A little jowly: there was a red line around his neck where the collar of

36

his cassock was too tight. A vain man, in his way, who liked to imagine he still had the slim body of a twenty-year-old. Everyone fell silent: the orphans, the ghosts, the bloody monks who haunted the corridors, shaking their chains. He took his place at the table.

'Good evening, children. Monseigneur Théas thanks you for your drawings' – he smiled at the little ones – 'and your letters' – a look at the older boys. 'He sends you his blessings. You may eat.'

His voice was soft. An alto's voice, incongruous coming from this baritone of a man. I pushed back my chair and walked up along the table in silence. A small boy stared at me, confused. Forty-two forks hung motionless in the air.

I may have been an atheist, but I was well brought up. I knew how to speak to a priest, even an intimidating one, dressed in a cassock. I knew where and when to call him 'Father'. He looked up at me, surprised. 'Good evening, Father. So, I got here yesterday … A temporary arrangement. I was just wondering if I could get a room of my own please, Father, and also would it be possible to have a salad as a starter? Nothing fancy, you know, just something a little bit healthier.'

Toad took a step towards me. The priest raised a finger and the school monitor froze.

'Why don't you read the Holy Word for us?'

That finger moved slightly and the little boy who had been reading walked away from the lectern and sat down. The priest looked at me. He was smiling. But his eyes … They could flush out sin. My parents' signatures, copied in my notebook. The money stolen from my mother's purse. Unthinkingly I obeyed him before he could see anything else. I read: 'But Stephen, full of the Holy Spirit, looked up to heaven.' I understood nothing of what I was reading. When I had finished the page, the priest signalled that I should continue. He did this again and again and by the time he announced: 'That's enough now,' I had already missed dessert and the table had been cleared. I had not eaten a thing.

The priest stood up, hands joined. Eighty-four other hands imitated his. Four hundred and twenty fingers intertwined to give thanks. *Peeep*. The line of boys moved towards the dormitory, except for those on washing-up duty.

'Not you,' the priest told me.

A distant *boom*.

He opened the Bible. Up close, he appeared shorter, darker. It was a darkness he cultivated – his hair was dyed. That ageless face, a handsome oval only slightly thickened by the overlarge jaw, was exactly the opposite of Rothenberg's, with its points and folds. And yet while the piano teacher was reassuring, the priest was disturbing. It was all in the eyes. Rothenberg's were all faded candour. The priest's were like a silver-grey blade.

He gestured towards a chair in the empty refectory.

'Do you know why you are here, at Les Confins?'

'My parents ...'

'Yes?'

'I have no parents any more.'

'You are mistaken.'

The priest pushed his open Bible towards me and pointed out a passage.

'Read this. Psalm 68:5.'

'"A father to the fatherless, a defender of widows, is God in his holy dwelling."'

'Continue.'

'"God sets the lonely in families, he leads out the prisoners with singing; but the rebellious live in a sun-scorched land."'

This sentence was underlined in pencil.

'The rebellious live in a sun-scorched land,' murmured the priest.

He sighed, placed a hand on my shoulder.

'I imagine you are hungry now?'

'Yes, Father. Very hungry.'

'Good. Feed on the Lord.'

That evening, for the first time in my life, I prayed. Back in the crypt, lying on bed 54, hands on my chest like all good recumbent statues, I called out from my kingdom of dust, my grey moon at the end of the world. And since my parents had not given me a god, since I could not talk to Beethoven – it would be rude to bother a genius over such a trifle – I addressed another hero, another god, whose job it was, perhaps, to listen to me.

This is bed 54. This is bed 54.

Do you read me, Colonel Michael Collins?

Michael Collins, the third man. The one whose name everybody forgot, the true hero of Apollo 11. While the others capered in slow motion for the television cameras, while confetti was being punched from sheets of paper 384,000 kilometres away, Michael Collins orbited the moon aboard the *Columbia*. He waited, in a cone of metal and Kapton speeding through space at 5,700 kilometres per hour, for the most delicate moment of the mission, the one the TV presenters had not talked about: the instant when he had to rendezvous with his colleagues, who were ascending from the lunar surface, at a point in space the size of a pinhead. The slightest error on his part – a loss of nerve, a momentary doubt, a miscalculation – and the *Columbia* would crash into the lunar module, or miss it completely. All that confetti would have been punched for nothing.

During each orbit, Michael Collins disappeared for forty-seven minutes. Just vanished into thin air, like a magic trick. During those forty-seven minutes he was flying over the dark side of the moon, with seventy-five billion trillion tons of grey rock between him and the earth. Forty-seven minutes when all communication was impossible. Forty-seven minutes of silence, forty-seven minutes of inky nothingness. A solitude greater than anything any man had known since Adam, as NASA would explain on 24 July 1969, in a message broadcast by every radio in the world.

This is bed 54. This is bed 54.

Do you read me, Colonel Michael Collins?

There was no answer from Michael Collins. Not that time.

Staff, dogsbodies, shadows. The employees at Les Confins, the cogs that kept this great machine running, from its infernal boiler to the slates on its roof, were us: the boarders. Mopping floors, chopping wood, washing dishes, cooking food. Weeding, laundry, polishing. Everything was organised to enable the orphanage to function with a minimum of external manpower. Each orphan had a daily chore to perform for a period of about two hours, between five and seven in the evening, no matter how young he might be.

At the head of the institution, Father Sénac taught most of the classes. Nor did he shirk the extra work unless called upon to celebrate Mass or administer the last rites to some clumsy oaf who had got in the way of a tractor. He could often be seen, the sleeves of his cassock rolled up to his elbows, chopping logs behind the outhouse, still a vigorous man in his sixties. Dominican nuns regularly came to visit us from a convent near Lourdes – an hour's drive away – for a few hours or a few days. Three of them had a permanent room at Les Confins. Sister Hélène taught mathematics. Sister Albertine was in charge of the kitchen, Sister Angélique the infirmary. If you ever passed one of them in the corridors, it was better to mutter a vague 'Hello, sister' rather than saying a name. In the black-and-white habits which revealed only their faces, they appeared more or less identical. Occasionally a novice would appear, a fresh convert never seen by any of us before, still trembling at her sacrifice. It never took long, however, for these new recruits to develop the hard-eyed stare that characterised true faith. Some of the nuns, such as Angélique, were kinder than others. But we did not delude ourselves. If Sénac had announced that all the orphans in the building were possessed by demons, the sisters would have poured petrol over us without a moment's hesitation, then fought each other to be first to the matches.

There were only three secular employees at Les Confins: Toad, the chief monitor; Étienne, the gardener; and Rachid, our PE teacher. My memories softened by time and distance, I would say that Toad was an absolute swine, a bastard, a piece of shit. Étienne was a surly, solitary man who spent his time gardening, mending fences, muttering incoherently and having epic drinking sessions in his cabin at the end of the garden. Rachid was a good person, and I am not saying that only because I once saw him beat the crap out of Toad. Or perhaps I am.

By the second morning, I had grasped the routine. The whistle blasts, the inspections, all the drama. Momo had returned from the infirmary and he avoided my gaze. The only new element came while Toad was walking along the rows of beds, apparently searching for something, and we heard him yell triumphantly from the other side of the velvet curtain that separated the little kids from the big kids. He reappeared, dragging a terrified Souzix by his ear, a wet and yellow-stained bedsheet hanging from his other fist like a hunting trophy. I lowered my eyes, and so did the others.

At breakfast, the priest walked behind Sister Albertine as she doled out slop. Hands behind his back, eyes ablaze with virtue, he sought out an unbuttoned collar, a creased shirt, a stained pair of shorts, anything that contravened the rules. When the cook came level with me, he gently put his hand out to stop her ladling the slop into my bowl.

'None for him.'

Sister Albertine walked past me. I was starving; this was the second meal I had missed. By chance, I caught the eye of the boy who slept under his bed – his nickname was Weasel – and he shot me a look that said: *Keep your mouth shut.*

As soon as the priest had moved away, someone touched my knee. Under the table, the boy next to me – a kid I did not know and would never get to know, because he left one month later – handed me half of his bread.

Among the pedagogical methods employed for our edification, one of the most common was known, among long-term residents of Les Confins, as the Cape of Piss. I witnessed this for the first time two days after my arrival. I was sitting by the window while Sister Hélène inflicted Pythagoras on her indifferent audience. Souzix walked through the courtyard, followed by Toad. The boy was naked, his urine-drenched sheet wrapped around him. His lips were blue. It was cold, this early in the morning, a thousand metres above sea level. He was the sorriest-looking superhero I had ever seen. He had to walk in circles around the courtyard, like a crestfallen Satan, until his sheet had dried. This would teach him a lesson, and if he did it again … well, clearly he was looking for trouble. At that point, they would really have to crack down.

Souzix came back to class after break, staring into space and ignoring the laughter and the cries of 'Pissssss!' that followed in his wake and rose to a crescendo before abruptly falling silent when the priest entered the room. Sénac handed back the previous day's test papers, pausing for a moment in front of Momo, who was drawing, before – without a word – giving him back his blank sheet. Then he turned to me, but did not give me my exam paper.

'My office. After class.'

He gestured at Souzix.

'Bring him with you.'

A dense silence descended upon the classroom. A few students stared at me curiously, not all of them wishing me well, drawn to the anticipation of another's misfortune like spectators at a bullfight. When the bell rang, Souzix walked ahead of me with the ample stride of an undertaker to a door on the first floor. He checked his clothes, then spat in his hand to flatten his hair. Just as he was about to knock, he changed his mind.

'Where are your parents?'

'They're dead.'

'Dead,' he repeated.

'Yeah,' I said. 'Deceased. Pushing up daisies. Dead.'

'What did they die of?'

'The abnormally elevated angle of incidence, combined with the underestimated speed and the presence of a strong crosswind, led the aircraft to stall.'

'Huh?'

'They exploded. Are you done asking questions now?'

'Were they strict?'

'A bit.'

'All the same,' Souzix murmured, shaking his head, 'parents shouldn't explode. Even if they are a bit strict.'

He knocked and the door creaked open to reveal an empty room. Souzix stood to attention by the door.

'We have to wait. Are you going to ask for Vercors this year?'

'Vercors?'

'It's the best holiday camp in the DDASS. Well, that's what I've heard anyway. I've never managed to go because everyone signs up for it. Sixty places for all the orphanages in France. Apparently there's a *swimming pool* with tractor tyres floating in it, and opposite the centre there's a *pizzeria*. I signed up again for next year, and the priest – Monsieur l'abbé, I mean – said I have a chance this time, if I keep my nose clean … Hey, where are you going?'

There it was, at the end of the room, under a high window. The first one I had seen in two months. An old upright piano, the wood unvarnished. A piano that had heard so many pleas, rages, false notes. A piano whose lid had been slammed shut in a fury, that had been ignored, moved from building to building and from wall to wall, that had gone out of tune and then been tuned, almost given away and then finally given away. A real piano.

I lifted up the lid. No dust on the keyboard.

'Don't touch it!' Souzix hissed. 'It belongs to the priest! Monsieur l'abbé,' he corrected himself, eyes wide with fear.

My fingers floated over the ivory. I didn't want to get into trouble. I fingered all the notes of Sonata no. 24, second movement – the last piece of homework Rothenberg had given me – without touching the piano. And, miraculously, I heard the music, clear and triumphant, just as surely as Beethoven had heard it.

'Bravo.'

The priest stood next to Souzix, one hand on the shoulder of the petrified boy. My fingers were sunk firmly in the keyboard. I had played so loudly that the final chord was still echoing inside the room. I swear I hadn't meant to press down on the keys. I had no memory of doing so. Muffled applause rose from the ground floor.

'I told him not to touch it ...'

The priest walked around his desk.

'You play very well.'

'No ... apparently I don't.'

'Who told you that?'

'Monsieur Rothenberg, my piano teacher.'

'Rothenberg. I see.'

I didn't see what he saw, as was often the case during my time there. Sénac took my test from his pocket and looked through it.

'Your essay, from yesterday. "Describe your most recent

meeting with God." You wrote a three-page letter to a certain ... *Collins*? Asking if you can meet him. There's something I'm missing here ...'

'He's an astronaut.'

'Ah. Now I understand that allusion to ... "the dark side of the moon", on the second page. Interesting.'

He put down my test paper and tapped his lips with two fingers.

'You believe yourself godless. A heretic, a troublemaker. But you are searching. You are calling. You're just like St John of the Cross – you know him? A very important mystic. He too was searching, through what he called his "dark night of the soul". Dark night of the soul, dark side of the moon ... you see where I'm going with this?'

No. I nodded.

'I've read your file, Joseph. I think you and I got off to a bad start. Since you use your fingers so well, I wonder if we can't put your talents to good use.'

'Of course, sir, thank you. Father. I play the piano, but I could also play the organ if I practised. I would need some scores, though, and—'

The priest gestured with his chin at a bulky typewriter that squatted on a desk. The letters HERMES 3000 on its grey hood – particularly the slight tilt of the *3000* – heralded the death of the fountain pen, promising its user a glorious future, a world of flying cars that would be piloted by humans without ink stains on their fingertips.

'Have you ever used one of these?'

'Never.'

He explained to me how the machine worked. Then he opened a leather Bible and dictated the first lines of Genesis. My piano-playing ability helped me become a more or less competent secretary within the hour.

'You are exempted from daily chores, with immediate effect. Every day, at five o'clock, you will come to my office and type up my letters. I am in constant correspondence with some important donors, the diocese, the management … You will save me a lot of time. But you must never touch anything in this office apart from the typewriter, you understand?'

'Not even the piano?'

'Especially not the piano. Give me your word.'

'I promise. But why?'

'When Pilate sentenced Jesus to crucifixion, do you think Christ asked him why?'

I had no idea what Christ might or might not have asked. From what little I knew of the story, though, I wouldn't have blamed him if he had asked that question. Perhaps it would all have been revealed as a big misunderstanding and disaster would have been averted. Afterwards, they might have laughed about it, over a bottle of good wine and some multiplied fish.

The priest started when he noticed that Souzix was still standing by the door, in the shadow of a cupboard.

'You're still here?'

'Yes, Monsieur l'abbé, I just wanted to say: it wasn't my fault that Joseph touched your piano.'

'Go. And close the door.'

'But about my holidays in Vercors …'

'I said go!'

Souzix went. The priest offered his hand, and when I reached out to shake it, he held mine in his grip.

'Many of our children come from difficult environments. They are rebels, stubborn fools. I see now that you are different. But beware the sin of pride. It has brought down greater men than you. Being my secretary does not mean you are superior to your classmates. On the contrary, this privilege makes you the smallest of the small. Let us remember the Saviour's words: "Whoever exalts himself will be humbled, and he who humbles himself will be exalted."'

'Amen,' said Souzix's voice from behind the door.

A wounded turtledove. My unbearable sister had found it in the forest where the hunters were shouting, just behind the Fourniers' manor house. Inès had cried out, and Henri and I had ignored her. Like good revolutionaries, we had just lit a Partagas cigar stolen from my father, and the revolution caused our heads to spin before making us feel like we were about to throw up. When my unbearable sister cried out a second time, I decided we ought to go and take a look.

The turtledove had fallen too far from the others, in dead silence. Nobody had picked it up. The hunters' saddlebags were already stuffed with birds, more than they could possibly eat. The dogs had already returned to the house. The 4×4s were setting off. The forest smelled of diesel and wine. The bird looked up at us, its body trembling. I wanted to touch it, to do something, but Inès stopped me.

'Your hands are dirty.'

She had been taught that it was wrong to touch something white, something fragile – our best tablecloth, Maman's Dior dresses, the car's cream seats – without washing your hands first, repeatedly rubbing the big bar of soap against your clumsy fingers until the water ran clear.

I hope that whoever picked up Inès, after she lost her wings, did not have dirty hands.

Every day, the priest dictated his letters to me. Sometimes we went beyond the allotted two hours. On those days, I would eat dinner later than the others, which made me an orphan of distinction. The others still didn't approach me, but at least they answered my questions now. My status as the priest's secretary gave them a vague respect for me. Or perhaps it was fear. At Les Confins, they were essentially the same thing.

One evening, Sénac caught me eyeing the piano, my fingers suspended over the keys of the Hermès 3000. If that piano was such a distraction, he said, he would have it removed. I wasn't there to play music.

'I didn't ask to be here,' I replied.

He turned slowly towards me. His eyes hit me, they assaulted me, and his hands shook very slightly. But when he spoke, his voice was calm.

'Nobody asked to be here. Type. "With my thanks, once again, for your generosity, dear sir, on behalf of the children and myself," and sign it "Your brother in Christ" … you know the rest.'

Quaking with indignation, I handed him the letter. He signed it, then waved me away without looking up.

Just as I was leaving the room, he said: 'Joseph.'

'Yes?'

He raised an eyebrow.

'Yes, Monsieur l'abbé?'

'Music can be a step towards God. The *last* step, to be taken when one is already very close. For you who are far from God, it is a distraction. A lure, a temptation.'

'But Beethoven—'

'Beethoven believed only in himself. And God, in his wisdom, decided that a man who didn't listen to him may as well end up deaf for all it would matter.'

That weekend, I made the acquaintance of the final employee at Les Confins. Rachid, the PE teacher, lived in a neighbouring village where he and his wife had taken over an old farm. In 1959, aged eighteen, he had participated in the first world championship for amateur bodybuilders. A somewhat stocky colossus, he had been relegated to twenty-second place in the competition – he had three classes a week with us. On Sunday, he often volunteered to accompany us on our weekly outing. We walked along the road in single file, Sénac leading and Toad bringing up the rear, singing psalms as we went. After three kilometres we were tempted away from the road by a path. We hiked up through the forest until we reached a mountain pasture surrounded by a cirque fashioned from the same granite as Les Confins, but open to the sky and bathed in sunlight, and I swear that what I felt in those moments was something close to joy. Rachid's wife, Camille, would sometimes come with us. She carried their baby, a newborn who knew everything – the Morocco of his father, the Brittany of his mother, all the skies piled up behind the one that we could see. He knew everything and was starting to forget it.

Sénac was a nature lover, and only the most extreme conditions would prevent us going on those outings. He had a typically Franciscan tenderness towards birds. We would often see him shedding a tear over a baby bird fallen from the nest, cheeping its distress. He would never let us pick up those baby birds, however, because 'God did not let it fall for no reason.' He never went out without a flaking metal telescope which he wore hanging from his neck by a leather strap and which he would suddenly point in one direction or another, muttering a barbarous-sounding name, to examine, eye glued to its lens, some feathered acrobats in which we had no interest. These were the only moments when we could ignore him and he didn't care.

That Sunday, one week after my arrival, Camille put her baby down in the grass. Forty-two wise men stood in a circle around her. Camille was wearing a flowered dress that revealed her legs and her vibrant chest. Indeed, her chest was so vibrant that it was almost too much to take, as I could see from the flushed, smiling faces around me, as I could feel from the pounding of my heart, the blood surging into forbidden parts. Rachid said nothing. He knew perfectly well that we were not going to wear Camille out just by looking at her. And even if he was wrong, and we did wear her out a little, there would still be plenty left for him.

Each boy there thought that he too would like one of those strange creatures one day – a baby. Or a girl like Camille to hold in his arms. Or the strength of Rachid. The mountain pasture was the only place where we ever thought: *tomorrow*. The possibility of the future never penetrated the thick walls of Les Confins.

Souzix stood sulking a little way off. Normally his tomfoolery made him the centre of attention and he was annoyed at being supplanted by this summertime Christ, this unvirginal Virgin. And for the first time in a long time, witnessing this second-hand Nativity, I felt good. My name was Joseph and I was where I belonged.

When the priest had had his fill of twisting his neck towards the sky, he snapped the telescope shut. Toad lifted Souzix up by his collar with one hand and shook him, pointing at his soil-stained shorts. Instead of kicking or protesting, Souzix just hung there limply like a pile of empty clothes, a technique I would quickly learn to master.

It was over.

The smaller boys had been exhausted by the outing to the mountain pasture. Some of them were already snoring when

Toad came into the dormitory, just after lights out. He took his strangely wide-set eyes and his amphibian pout on a journey through the darkness, seeking out transgressions between the beds: a pair of unaligned shoes that might trip him up, a badly closed trunk, a boy who was crying out of fear or fatigue or whatever, a boy who would then be dragged from the bed so that the chief monitor could give the little brat a good reason to cry.

Toad's past was the subject of endless speculation. The vampire theory, promulgated by Souzix, had been set aside when someone else had pointed out that he had a reflection, he wore a crucifix around his neck, and he was rather fat for a creature that supposedly fed only on blood, particularly the blood of orphans. Other theories suggested that the priest had met him in a prison where he used to be the chaplain, and had hired him once he was freed. That he dismembered children for pleasure. As far as I know, Toad never dismembered anyone, not at Les Confins anyway. It wasn't his type of torture: the suffering would not have lasted long enough. Toad was a connoisseur of suffering: he liked it to be aged over many years, with a long finish, the kind of suffering he could sip from time to time, smacking his lips in delight, satisfied in the knowledge that he was not about to run short of this particular vintage. Others believed that Toad was a former student at Les Confins. This theory, at least, was false. Later, I checked the register of all the children who had passed through that institution after its conversion from a priory to an orphanage in 1936 – and his name was not among them. One last rumour, the most plausible of all, had it that he was a former legionnaire. He walked with a slight limp, which gave credence to the theory of a war wound, and then there was the military song that he once forced me to sing along with him. And he certainly knew how to hit where it hurt but would not leave a mark. One small kid who accidentally strayed into Toad's attic room said he had not seen anything strange there, but what would seem strange to a boy who still believed in Father Christmas? There were many other legends about our chief monitor, of course. That Toad could not feel pain. That his back was covered in scales, that he spoke unknown languages. That one day he had received a black-edged envelope, had gone up to his room to read the letter inside, and had come out again with red eyes. But nobody really believed such nonsense.

Boom.

I was used to the noise by now. Maybe it was a distant quarry or mine, although that did not explain the oppression in my eardrums and my chest, the impression I had that, for a brief instant, a passageway had opened up to another world. I had no idea how true that would turn out to be.

Despite his best efforts, Toad did not find any misdemeanours. He limped out of the dormitory, leaving behind him a heady trail of sweat and disappointment. Weasel, my neighbour, slipped under his bed. He looked at me and put a finger to his lips – *shhh* – just as he had on my first night, a week before. In a place like that, a gesture that was repeated had to be either a ritual or a threat. I closed my eyes.

When I opened them again, the moon had moved, clearing the way for a whole new batch of darkness. My neighbour's bed was empty, both above and beneath. And yet we were not allowed to get up for any reason, on pain of I wasn't sure what, but something bad anyway. Four figures – one small, three taller – were sneaking between the beds towards the door. I did my very best to resist. I imagined Toad inflicting a thousand different punishments and tortures upon me, imagined him lurking there somewhere in the darkness, watching and waiting for me to step out of line so he could make an example of me. But, in the end, curiosity got the better of me. I followed them.

'Hey, you, fifty-four!'

A head emerged from under a blanket just as I was about to

leave the dormitory. A blond boy, about twelve years old, his gaze adrift upon a pale ocean.

'You should go back to bed,' he whispered.

'Where are they going?'

'No idea. But those kids are always in trouble.'

His head vanished under the blanket. I did what any fifteen-year-old would do when given a piece of advice, especially good advice: I ignored it.

The corridor was empty. Guided by a draught, I groped my way towards a half-open door. Just then, Sénac came around the corner. He passed within a few feet of me but did not see me – I have no idea why not – then unlocked another door, went through it and closed it behind him. This second door was metal and covered in flaking blue paint, so different from all the others that I almost followed the priest instead. But the oak door I had pressed against yawned open and I continued on my way, completely unaware at that moment that these two doors led to the same story.

A spiral staircase ascended between forgotten walls. The draught grew stronger. At the top, a cast-iron trapdoor. Four faces stared at me in amazement when I pushed it open: Souzix and the three older boys that he always hung around with and whose names I had now learned. Weasel, Edison, Sinatra. All four of them were sitting in the middle of a tiled terrace – an anomaly in this world of slopes. Around them rose the ocean-liner chimneys of the old priory, while the impressive slate decks pitched, black and glistening, edged with zinc guard rails.

'What the hell are you doing here, fifty-four?' Weasel demanded, turning off the portable radio, a Telefunken, over which they had all been leaning.

'My name is Joe. And what about you – what are *you* doing?'

'None of your business. Go back to bed.'

I hoisted myself up onto their terrace and felt suddenly dizzy: the sky was there, vast enough that I might topple head first into it. There was never much of a view from Les Confins. From here, you could see other worlds.

'Where are we?'

'The Lookout. It's a secret society, and you're not a member. So piss off.'

'A secret society. What are you, nine?'

'Yes,' said Souzix in a serious voice.

'And what do you do in this "secret society"?'

'We keep watch over the world. We protect Les Confins.'

'From what?'

'Russians,' said Sinatra.

'The Mafia,' added Edison.

'And giants,' Souzix concluded.

I laughed. 'And has the orphanage ever been attacked by Russians, mobsters or giants?'

Weasel climbed to his feet and stood directly in front of me.

'No. And you know why? Because of us. I guard the north, Edison the south, Sinatra the east.'

'I'm too small to be a guard,' added Souzix. 'I can't see over the parapet.'

'So who guards the west?'

All four of them lowered their eyes.

'It was Danny.'

'And where is this Danny?'

'He's dead.'

'How did he die?'

'Does it matter, how he died? The effect's the same, isn't it? Now go back to bed.'

'Wait, so Toad lets you leave the dormitory?'

I learned more that night than in a lifetime at Les Confins. In fact, I didn't learn much after that, apart from the existence of an infinite evil. But also of a sweetness for which I was willing to bear anything.

Weasel, the guard of the north, was fifteen. Ten years earlier he had been dug from the ruins of an apartment building in Marseille that had simply collapsed in on itself one day with a long sigh of plaster after years spent fighting gravity, logic, neglect. It had been in the newspapers. All of its forty-five inhabitants had died – all except Weasel, whose father had just had time to throw him under a bed when the building gave up the ghost. Weasel received a package every month (from whom? from where? we would never find out) stuffed full of various sweets and knick-knacks. Some distant aunt or cousin, beyond the horizon, easing their conscience? This manna enabled Weasel to remain at the centre of all the orphanage's trafficking deals. He traded, swapped, lent, as eagerly as any loan shark. If one of his debtors did not pay for a favour, or missed a deadline, Sinatra punished him. Weasel had Étienne, the gardener, more or less in his pocket because he gave him the proceeds of his trafficking: money. In exchange, Étienne invited Toad to his cabin every Sunday evening to watch television, leaving the way clear for The Lookout. If anything went wrong, Étienne would flash the lights in the tiny outhouse behind his cabin. There had been only one such alarm in several years – a *false* alarm – which happened one night when Toad, having been overcome by violent diarrhoea after eating Étienne's cooking, had emptied his bowels in a series of urgent spasms, with one hand on the light switch.

Fourteen-year-old Edison was the genius of the group. The radio that they were listening to that night was his creation: he had built it using a broken old radio set they had found in a skip during a rare outing to the village. It worked with homemade batteries that Edison had fabricated using old coins, vinegar, and cardboard and metal washers. The world would not be the same had Edison lived longer, I feel sure of it. And perhaps he would have lived longer had he not been cursed with what, for a genius, were crippling flaws. First, he was an orphan. Second, and most importantly, he was not perfectly white – his mother was Senegalese. Toad had several times taken pleasure in sending him back under the shower in the morning on the pretext that he was 'still dirty'. Fortunately for Edison, Toad had another whipping boy. Unfortunately for Souzix, it was him.

Despite being only nine – and the guard of nothing at all – Souzix was the doyen of The Lookout because he was the only one among us to have been born an orphan. To be more specific, he was born with no name – his mother choosing to mark his birth certificate with an X where his name should have been so that the French State would take him into its care. *Né sous X*: he had heard this phrase so many times that he had taken its phonetic pronunciation for his own name, Souzix. The product of a one-night stand, this small boy was drawn to older kids at the orphanage and, because of his seniority, they accepted him. Souzix talked about the little kids in his own section with contempt, calling them 'brats'. The only things that betrayed his age, other than his size, were his passion for *Mary Poppins* and those nights when he would wake up with a pillow wet from tears – and his sheets wet for another reason. And the mornings after, when he would have to wear the Cape of Piss in the snow, the Cape of Piss in the sun, the Cape of Piss until he could take no more, although that was not enough to prevent it happening again and again, to Toad's delight.

Sinatra was the last member of The Lookout. A force of nature, a handsome slim boy encased within a thick layer of fat. How he managed that, given our meagre daily diet, was a mystery. He was sixteen but looked closer to twenty, and he claimed to be the love child of the famous American crooner. His mother had told him that the great Frank had got lost one stormy, drunken night with his orchestra during a French tour. She had taken him in, one thing had led to another, and they had sung together, nestled close to the fire, to the rhythm of the rain – that damned rhythm again! Our Sinatra was born from a voice, from a storm, perhaps from madness, since his mother had been committed to an asylum after being found dancing naked in the village square. Whenever anyone talked to him about this episode, or how unlikely it seemed that Frank Sinatra would have slept with a shopkeeper from Figeac, or even set foot in the region, our friend's natural placidity would dissolve into an impressive rage. Sinatra sent his 'father' unaddressed letters, convinced that they would reach him and Ol' Blue Eyes would come to France and rescue him. But they must never have been delivered, because no one came. So, he said, he would leave one day. He would go to Las Vegas.

'What will you do when you get there?' Souzix kept asking him. 'Prospect for gold?'

'Gold is worthless in America. They have so much of it that they use it to pave the streets.'

And Souzix's eyes would widen, filled with yellow dreams.

Boom. Louder this time, up here in this fresh, unresisting air, reverberating over the rooftops. The time had come: I had to know.

'What is that noise?'

'What noise?'

They had been hearing it for so long that they had forgotten it, like the passing of time, like their own breathing, and even though I described it, insistently, none of them seemed to know what I was talking about. I had to wait until the next day before I finally received an explanation. An explanation that I initially found disappointing, since I could not gauge its importance.

I was about to turn back, return to the dark depths of my orphanage, when Edison leapt towards their DIY radio.

'Battle stations!'

Souzix gave a yelp of excitement and ran to the transistor radio. The volume knob was turned up all the way and the little box kept spitting out long bursts of static and whistling modulations.

'What's going on?' asked Weasel.

'A Russian nuclear missile is headed straight for Les Confins.'

'Start the destruction process.'

Fingers on the buttons, Edison dived into the froth of radio waves that the world had sent crashing onto our rooftop.

'Command frequency acquired ...' The others waited, eyes to the sky. Souzix was barely even breathing. Suddenly a shooting star drew a line through the night and Edison announced: 'Missile intercepted.'

I was about to laugh at these childish games when my eyes met Weasel's. As usual, they ordered me to remain silent, but the *shhh* this time was harder, firmer, and afterwards they stared meaningfully at Souzix. The kid's head was thrown back and he was looking up at the sky, a sky full of stars that rolled over his cheeks, a world of thwarted threats, of galaxies with the long hair of a mother. Nobody believed in those missiles, except him. The other three were protecting his fragile naivety, having lost it themselves one fine morning without ever really knowing how. The Lookout was not a game, it was a conspiracy. A sleight of hand, a mangy-looking rabbit pulled from a hat by a group of amateur magicians for a nine-year-old boy. And as any musician will tell you, it is harder to perform for one person than for thousands. It is rare that you will disappoint thousands.

'Okay, I want to become a member of your society. What do I have to do?'

'Just ask,' said Weasel.

'That's it?'

'Yep.'

'All right then, I ask to become a member of The Lookout.'

'Request denied.'

Despite being almost sixteen, despite not having shed a tear over anything since my parents had been incinerated in a massive ball of fire, I felt like I was about to cry.

'Why?'

'Because you're Sénac's minion,' said Sinatra, taking a comb from his pocket and tidying his hair. 'That's why.'

'I'm not Sénac's minion!'

'You're teacher's pet, his mascot, his little choirboy. We don't need any minions here.'

I threw myself at Sinatra. I had learned to fight from my physical training manual, in which the illustrations showed the adversary pummelled with onomatopoeic blows. Sinatra had learned to fight in the street. He had the reach of an American boxer and he knocked me to the floor. For an instant I saw him floating above me, fists balled like Cassius Clay – *Sonny Liston is down, he's trying to get back on his feet* – the umpire counting; I had watched that bout with Papa against Maman's wishes – *it's too violent for him, no, it's fine, darling, he's big enough to see this,* one two three, *look, son, this is a victory for the oppressed, the little people, the outcasts*, a taste of rubber in my mouth, the smell of the ring, a rigged fight, blood, seven eight nine, Edison holding back Sinatra who wanted to finish the job, the distant *boom*, the roar of the crowd, ten, I lost consciousness.

When she was still alive, my grandmother, the Englishwoman, used to say: I don't understand you French people with your genders. You get the masculine and feminine all mixed up. You're blind to the beauty of la, *you celebrate the boredom of* le. *For example, you say* une voiture *for a car. But surely such a dull, cubic object should be* un. *Whereas you say* un baiser *for a kiss, a miracle that can last a lifetime. You should say* une baiser. 'Il m'a donné une baiser dans le voiture' *– that's much more beautiful, don't you think?*

'Hey, fifty-four, wake up!'

My grandmother also used to say: there are two things in life that I love: lying and gardening. I love lying so much that I've just done it: I hate gardening. Lying is much more useful. Remember that, Joseph.

'He's babbling about his granny. I told you you hit him too hard.'

'What are you talking about? I barely even touched him.'

I never really knew my grandmother. She lied to the doctor who asked her if it hurt when he was palpating her breasts during the annual check-up. She said it didn't, because having one's breasts palpated was not the done thing for a good Englishwoman: everyone knew where that might lead. The fact that it was for medical reasons made no difference. So she told him no, hiding the pain in her right breast behind the stiff upper lip that built an empire; no, she did not feel any pain at all. A few months later, she was dead. I was six. Maman explained to me what had killed my grandmother. For years afterwards, I was afraid that my mother's breasts would kill her too.

'Maman!'

I opened my eyes. I was sitting on my bed, covered in sweat. The boys from The Lookout watched me with relief. They must have carried me down there from the roof.

'See? What did I tell you? I barely even touched him.'

My eye was throbbing. I wasn't sure that I had cried out 'Maman!'; it might easily have been someone else. You got used to those *mamans* yelled, whispered, moaned, hugged in great armfuls of nothing in the middle of the night; they were like rain pattering against the windowpane. To my right, Weasel slipped under his bed. To my left, Momo stared into the darkness with his eternal smile, as if sensing something funny in all the drama. Now that I think about it, I'm not sure I ever saw Momo asleep. He must have slept, though, at least during those black deviations that seized him sometimes, short-circuited him, making his body shake so hard that Sister Angélique had to shove a piece of wood in his mouth to prevent him biting his tongue and choking. Momo nodded and I looked away. He disgusted me with his words that never came out. He disgusted me with his bushy eyebrows and his vacant eyes in which I could not yet make out the blue of Oran, the gold of deserts, the whole shimmering palette of Algeria, so beautiful that so many had wished to possess it.

I was, I confess, no saint. The boys in The Lookout even less so, although they had an excuse. When you see a child staggering under the weight of a schoolbag or an old man struggling to drag along a suitcase, you rush over to help them. But these kids — I call them kids but, with the exception of Souzix, they were almost men — had been carrying their anger around for years and nobody had ever offered to help them with it. People turned a blind eye as they stumbled over kerbs. Who cared if they fell? It was better than being crushed by what they were carrying.

They were tough, they were funny, they had never won at anything.

My friends.

On sad evenings, on evenings of sour wine, I still think about them.

'What was that?' Rothenberg groaned.

Fingers pinching the bridge of his nose. Motionless. A statue of despair.

'What was it?' he repeated.

I recognised the expression on his face. And yet I thought I'd played well.

'The first movement of Sonata no. 14, also known as the "Moonlight Sonata".'

'That's not what you played. What you played was a monstrosity. Explain yourself.'

'I was thinking about Aline,' I admitted, blushing.

'Who?'

'A girl from school. I was thinking about her, to find the right atmosphere.'

'The right atmosphere?'

'Yeah ... you know, romantic. Walking in the moonlight with someone you like ...'

Rothenberg blew his top, as if he had just been waiting for this moment. Well, he *had* just been waiting for this moment – he had taught whole generations of imbeciles before me.

'Romantic? What you played was *schmaltz*! It was oozing out of your fingertips. Look, it's all over the carpet! Mina!' he yelled. 'Mina! Do you want some *schmaltz* to put on the chips? Joe's produced tons of the stuff – thick, greasy goose fat, it's dripping everywhere! Bring the basin!'

'Calm down, Alon,' Madame Rothenberg replied from upstairs.

'It's Joseph,' I corrected him. 'Not Joe.'

'Joseph is the name of the Messiah's father, or the name of a great musician. You are neither.'

Let the storm pass. Rothenberg's rages were legendary. They drew on an indignation beyond his own life, on three thousand years of affronts.

'Did I ask you to prepare this piece – yes or no?'

'Yes, Monsieur Rothenberg. And I did.'

'What did you do?'

'I studied the score.'

'You only looked at the score? You started with the first bar, without wondering what came before?'

'There was something before?'

I picked up my score and examined it from every angle, thinking that perhaps the first pages were stuck together. Rothenberg slapped the back of my head.

'You didn't read Ludwig's letters to his friend Franz Wegeler, for instance? No, don't bother answering – I've heard enough from you. I heard your mouth and I heard your fingers and I can't stand any more of their stupidity! There is no moonlight, you understand? No, I told you not to reply! There is no moonlight – that was just a nickname some cretin gave the sonata thirty years later. In 1801, when Ludwig wrote this piece, it had nothing to do with the moon, you understand?'

I did not speak. He slapped the back of my head again.

'You understand? Answer me, you idiot! Cat got your tongue?'

'No. I mean, no, I don't understand.'

'Of course you don't understand, because you didn't read Ludwig's letters to his friend Franz Wegeler! If you'd read them, you would know that by that point Ludwig had already lost most of his hearing and that he hadn't told anyone except a few close friends. The Adagio in no. 14 is not a moonlight promenade. It's a *funeral march*. A lament. What you hear is the sound of a genius going deaf!'

Rothenberg, out of breath, stopped speaking for a moment.

'Play it again. And think about the position of your hands, for God's sake. Imagine you are holding oranges.'

I obeyed, but I was so rattled that I played two false notes in the first five bars before giving up.

'I can't, Monsieur Rothenberg. My hands are shaking.'

'Finally,' replied my old teacher.

'Show me that eye.'

My fingers froze above the typewriter keys. *With my sincere gratitude, Monseign*—Even the Hermès 3000 held its breath. Sénac lifted up my chin. And yet I'd been so careful to keep my face down when I entered. This trick had worked with Toad, to whom I had, with Egyptian cunning, offered my unmarked profile all day long. Sénac examined the yellow circle around my left eye, the consequence of its encounter with Sinatra's right hand.

'Have you been fighting?'

'No, I slipped in the shower.'

The priest sat facing me.

'You know you can tell me anything, don't you? Violence among the boys is unacceptable. Just give me a name.'

I was tempted to confess everything. To tell him about those bastards who didn't want me in their secret society.

'If someone did this to you, I want to know.'

'I fell in the shower.'

'You're sure?'

'Yes.'

'I beg your pardon?'

'Yes, Monsieur l'abbé.'

He leaned towards me, smiling smoothly.

'You're absolutely certain that's what happened?'

'Yes, Monsieur l'abbé.'

His smile did not waver, it only tensed a little. He picked up his telephone, murmured 'Monsieur Marthod please,' into the receiver. A few moments later, Toad arrived, breathing heavily.

'You wanted to see me, Monsieur l'abbé?'

'Joseph here slipped in the shower this morning. The safety of the young people in our care is your responsibility. You will scrub the bathroom from top to bottom to make sure there is not a single trace of any slippery residue.'

'Now?' the monitor asked, incredulous.

'Of course now. You will also clean the dormitory, as an act of penitence. Cleanliness is next to godliness, after all. Do not come to dinner – that would be a waste of your precious time. When you have finished, come and find me. I will hear your confession. We will ask the Lord to grant us the necessary vigilance and to harden our hearts against the sin of complacency.'

Toad turned pale at these words. His admiration for Sénac was boundless. According to an apocryphal but persistent story, one of the nuns had been heard to say that Toad 'owed everything to the priest'. For a moment he looked hurt.

'I don't want to hear about any more incidents of this kind, Monsieur Marthod. Please ensure that Joseph has no cause for complaint in the future.'

Toad turned to me. For the first time, I noticed that he did not really have any eyebrows. His face sloped gently down from forehead to chin, emasculating itself in a pair of soft lips that quivered beneath his green, round amphibian gaze.

'I'll see to it, Monsieur l'abbé, I'll see to it. You can trust me.'

He kissed the crucifix that he wore around his neck and patted me on the shoulder before leaving. The priest put on his coat.

'Now, where were we? Ah, yes: "and my wishes for a speedy recovery. Your brother in Christ", et cetera, you know the rest. Tidy up behind me, please – I must run. I am celebrating Mass at Sainte-Marie tonight. Oh, and please go down to see Étienne before returning to your dormitory. Tell him that the front gate does not shut properly and that he should fix it tomorrow morning at the earliest opportunity.'

'Monsieur l'abbé?'

'Yes, Joseph?'

'Is Christ our brother?'

'Of course.'

'But if Christ is my brother, why am I here? Why did he let this happen?'

'Jesus did not save himself. Why would he save you?'

'Because I didn't do anything wrong!'

'Even if that were true, even if you had not been sullied by the weakness of Adam and the arrogance of Eve, have you thought about your parents? Did they do nothing wrong either? What do you know of their sins? Believe me, if you're here, there is a reason. God is not cruel.'

God is no airline pilot, that's for sure. Even so, what would it have cost him to overshoot the runway while the pilot wasn't looking so he could try the approach a second time, or to lower the plane's nose by a few degrees? The Caravelle wouldn't have stalled. My parents would have come home, and my unbearable sister and I would have quarrelled just as we always did. Maybe she and I wouldn't even be talking to each other by now. We would have fallen out over some stupid inheritance issue. We wouldn't have been best buddies, but that's life.

So yes, for a long time I believed that God was cruel. A sadist.

And then one day, while playing a sonata, I understood. Hadn't it occurred to anyone that God was perhaps, quite simply, deaf as a post? That he was already hard of hearing when his son called out: *Eli, Eli, lama sabachthani*, why have You forsaken me? Maybe he didn't forsake anyone. Maybe he saw his child's pale lips moving, down there on the cross, but he didn't understand what he was saying. That whole story – the crucifixion and what came after: the skyscraping cathedrals, the controversies, the heretics burned at the stake, the fingernails torn off and the haloes handed out (often to the same people) – maybe it was just one gigantic misunderstanding.

If God is deaf, we must forgive Him. Forgive him whole-heartedly for our wounded days and our crippled hearts.

On the way to Étienne's cabin, I ran into Souzix in the covered courtyard. He was strolling along, hands behind his back, looking very serious, like a wise old man. Only his enormous shadow, cast onto the wall by the courtyard searchlight, revealed him in his true light.

'What was that music, Joseph?'

'What music?'

'The tune you were playing the other day, on the priest's piano.'

'It was ... I'd like to tell you, but I can't.'

'Why not?'

'Because you're not part of *my* secret society.'

Souzix accepted my vengeance without protest and went on his way, following the Way of the Cross to which I had just added another station. Suddenly I felt bad.

'Hang on! It was Beethoven. Sonata no. 24, "À Thérèse".'

He came back towards me and stared up at me like a little professor.

'What's a sonata?'

'It's a kind of ... a musical letter.'

'And who was this Thérèse woman?'

'Ugh, you and your questions! What difference does it make who she was?'

'Well, if I wrote a letter to Mary Poppins, it would be sweet and loving. But if I wrote to Suzanne, who was my adoptive mother and who I didn't like very much, it would not be sweet or loving. So how can you play your letter if you don't know who you're writing to?'

Souzix. I want to believe that one day someone will sense your presence, for a brief instant, in the soft flesh of a summer evening, in the substance of the world. And that, if they search really hard, they will feel a little Souzix-shaped hollow.

Trains. The supersonic boom came from simple trains. Étienne explained it all to me when I went to give him the priest's message. He knew what he was talking about: he had worked on that railway before becoming Les Confins's resident handyman.

'Let's wait for the next one. You'll see. Do you smoke? I won't tell the Crow.'

'Who's that?'

'Sénac, you idiot.'

He handed me a Gitane, which I wedged behind my ear as I'd seen the older boys do outside my old school. A railway line ran alongside the lowest terrace of the orphanage, without any separation at all. Both of them – the trains on one side and the orphans on the other – belonged to the French State, and as long as the latter didn't fall under the former, why waste money on a fence? The track disappeared into a tunnel, only a dozen feet from Étienne's cabin.

'It's coming. Listen to the rails sing. We call that the lullaby.'

The beast was rising, its orange eyes full of the fog that covered the north-facing slope even in the middle of summer. The headlights wept, leaving behind long amber streaks, the tracks of its tears.

'It's speeding up,' Étienne explained. 'That damn tunnel is so narrow that if you're not going exactly eighty kilometres per hour when you enter it, you graze the sides because of the oscillation. And the suits in Paris shave the difference off your pay.'

The locomotive dived into the mountain, thirty or so carriages rumbling behind it. Pregnant with metal and wood, with petrol and milk, cement, cars, aeroplane parts, modernity. A major part of the trade between north and south passed through here, clogging up this route which had not been designed for such a volume of traffic. It linked France to Spain, Le Havre to Tangier, the North Atlantic to the Mediterranean.

'Five kilometres hollowed out with pickaxes and dynamite by queers, kikes, Basques and poets,' Étienne explained. 'Everyone who Franco hated. We would call them slaves; they called them political prisoners. They're building a more modern link on the Aragnouet side, but it keeps running into problems. We'll be dead before they finish that.'

Men, women and families regularly attempted to flee Franco's Spain through the old tunnel. It was impossible. Five kilometres long and nowhere to hide when a train went through. A few centimetres at most between the carriages and the walls, and the driver had to be perfectly in control to keep the train running straight. Inside the tunnel, it was blacker than night; even the headlights gave up. On both sides, the French and the Spanish, a line of convoys was permanently waiting at the switch point. When one left, another entered, travelling in the opposite direction, every thirty minutes. Anyone who attempted to escape on foot was doomed. Étienne swore that the tunnel walls were red with the blood of all the imbeciles who had tried it. So, on the whole, it was probably better that it was too dark to see anything. He himself, when he was driving, had several times felt suspicious bumps, unexplained jolts.

'You didn't think about it. You just did your job.'

We watched as the last carriage disappeared. Less than ten seconds later, *boom*, a palmful of pure air smacked me in the chest. Étienne started laughing.

'See? There's not much space between the train and the walls, so the locomotive shoves the air forward in front of it. The pressure up ahead increases – you can feel it on the windows, believe me, everything starts to vibrate. This creates a hollow behind. But nature abhors a vacuum – you must have learned that at school, right? So the air ends up escaping through every crack it can find, at the sides, above, below, it rushes along the train and the pressure suddenly equalises behind the convoy. That's the noise you hear. Because of the way the valleys are shaped you also hear the sound on the Spanish side, reverberating over here. If you pay attention, you'll notice it doesn't sound exactly the same.'

'But ... doesn't it keep you awake at night?'

Étienne took a hip flask from his pocket.

'When you're my age, you'll be afraid of silence, not noise. Anyway, off you go now. Tell the Crow that I'll fix his front gate tomorrow morning, even if I don't see why it's so urgent. Actually, don't tell him that last bit. You'd better hurry. There's a storm coming.'

Étienne returned to his cabin, but I did not go back straight away. Big clouds were rolling over the mountain peaks. The thunder cleared its throat and the grass shivered. All day long, I'd had a strange feeling, as if this was no ordinary day. I felt as if some fundamental right had been flouted, as if I had been refused what ought to be mine, and yet I would have sworn that I had nothing left for them to take. And when I realised what it was, I started laughing, all alone, laughing until I could hardly breathe as I wandered through the crisp grass from one terrace to another. Of course – it was the date. The twenty-eighth of July 1969. There *was* something else they could take from me.

My birthday. Sixteen years since my mother had given birth to me during the night at a private hospital in Saint-Mandé, cursing, panting, forcing my father to swear, as she crushed his hand in hers, that they would never do it again, and perhaps that perjury was the sin for which they had to atone. The priest was right – what did I know of my parents' sins?

The sky opened up and shed fat, hot drops of rain. They

smelled of hay and holidays. The darkness was thick enough to chew. I lifted my face so I could breathe in the storm, fill my lungs.

Toad didn't give me time to do it.

I hadn't heard him approaching. He immobilised me with a skilful armlock and held an old oil-scented handkerchief over my mouth. The storm intensified. It would have been simpler not to struggle – Toad was too strong. Even so, I did struggle, out of principle, out of habit, just like all the others he must have killed before me in other monsoons. Others who had also failed to hear him sneaking through the ferns and the palms, others who had thought themselves safe. My field of vision was filled with bleeding jellyfish, tumours floating inside my lungs. My tongue, my teeth searched for air. But nothing passed through – not a trickle, not an atom, just a vile taste of grease and snot. Toad was a virtuoso.

Bed 54, this is Columbia, *I've detected a problem with your oxygen feed.*

Michael Collins? Is that you?

You called me, didn't you?

The other day, yes, but I thought you hadn't heard me.

I heard you. Hit him. Use your fists, your feet, whatever you want, but aim low.

My fist hit something soft, my heel a tibia. Toad grunted with pain. And suddenly I could breathe. Grass against my cheek. Les Confins lay before me, sideways, the landscape upside down. Breathe. A few centimetres away, a dung beetle was slaloming between drops of rain. I wanted to get up, make the world level again. A foot between my shoulder blades kept me pinned to the ground.

The sound of a belt buckle, a zipper being unfastened. Hot

liquid splashing over my legs, the smell of ammonia mingling with that of wet earth.

'Next time,' said a distant voice, 'watch what you say and who you say it to.'

Toad shook the last drops onto me, zipped his trousers up, and strode heavily away.

When I opened my eyes again, I was running. In a darkness worthy of Genesis, the first day, the pitch black that preceded light, when there was nothing but the abyss, water and the spirit of God. And, once again, I asked to see God. The rain was pounding down even harder. Putting out all my fires, washing the earth from my hair, the mud from my face, Toad's urine from my clothes. I didn't know where I was. But I had to run – of that, I felt sure. A terrifying cold was pursuing me, its breath on the back of my neck.

Stop, son. You'll catch pneumonia.

No, Michael Collins. You're just a voice in my head.

Many men have a voice in their head. The cunning ones make money out of it. Now, please, stop running.

I'm not crazy. I studied the Apollo 11 flight plan with my father. I read everything about you, Neil and Buzz. I know you should be back on earth now. You can't be speaking to me. It's impossible.

See? You're doing it again. Your old teacher, Rothenberg, was right: you don't listen. What does it matter where I am? I'm speaking to you. That's all that counts.

Just let me run, Michael Collins. If I stop, the cold will catch me. Nobody can help me. I'm all alone.

Don't make me laugh, my boy. You want me to tell you how it feels to be alone? Truly alone? Shall I tell you about the anxiety that gripped me when the Columbia *went behind the moon during each orbit? When night cut off the radio link that connected me to the rest of humanity? Do you have any idea of the monsters that live there, on the other side of the craters?*

Sorry, Michael Collins. I didn't mean to make you angry. Papa said you were the real hero of that mission. That it took nerves of steel to pilot the *Columbia*.

Forget nerves of steel. This is what I wanted to tell you, on your birthday. Our little secret, because you're an astronaut too, in your own way. You know how I made it through, each time I went behind the moon? How I survived the crushing silence and darkness? I knew. I knew that the Columbia *would ultimately emerge into the light. It's a question of orbit. Believe me, I know this from experience: the worst loneliness lasts only forty-seven minutes.*

Somewhere in the archives of the Gendarmerie Nationale, you will perhaps find the account of that night, the night of my sixteenth birthday. To be more specific, you will have to visit the historical department in La Défense and ask for the case files of the 4th regional command unit for the Midi-Pyrénées, the gendarmerie group for the Hautes-Pyrénées, and – more specifically still – the gendarmerie in Lourdes. If the archives have not been burned or lost or stolen or damaged, you will be able to consult an official report.

It should say this:

Report by Gendarme Louviers, 31 July 1969

At approximately 22:15 on 28 July 1969, we received a call from the institution 'Les Confins', which belongs to the Departmental Directorate of Sanitary and Social Affairs and is run by the Diocese of Tarbes, informing us that one of their boarders had run away. At 23:00, Staff Sergeant Cazaux and I picked up a young man wandering along the road to Lourdes. Visibly disorientated, he identified himself as 'Joseph Marty, orphan and astronaut', before falling unconscious. He had been running in the rain for an hour and had covered a distance of approximately eight kilometres. Staff Sergeant Cazaux and myself, after a telephone consultation with the institution 'Les Confins', and noting that he was not injured, decided to take the young man to the gendarmerie. During the interrogation, Joseph Marty told us that he had been assaulted by a man known as 'Toad', the chief monitor of the orphanage. This assault had led him to run away. He was able to escape due to the fact that the front gate did not close properly.

Within one hour, Father Armand Sénac, the director of 'Les Confins', came in person to pick up the young man. Joseph Marty had the beginnings of a fever and he offered no resistance to this development. Confronted with the young man's accusations, Father Sénac, whose charitable actions and devotion are well known throughout the department, explained to us that Joseph Marty was a new arrival, psychologically fragile and still very shaken by his parents' death. According to him, such accusations were typical of young people seeking attention while in a situation of extreme emotional distress. He invited us to investigate for ourselves at our convenience.

The next day, we went to the institution 'Les Confins'. We were welcomed warmly by the orphans and staff. The students, questioned in groups and then individually, in accordance with protocol, assured us that they had never been mistreated. They all seemed highly appreciative of their spiritual director, as well as the chief monitor Marthod ("Toad'), described by the children as 'a really nice guy' and by the Dominican nuns who work at 'Les Confins' as 'strict but fair'. Monsieur Marthod stated that he was not angry with young Marty and that he understood the distressing nature of his situation. Monsieur Marthod also asked us to pass on his greetings to Colonel Lafitte, at command headquarters in Bordeaux.

In light of:

• the plaintiff's lack of credibility;

• the absence of any injuries on the plaintiff's body;

• the general esteem in which the management of the institution is held, the theory that this was the

The fever lasted eleven days. A doctor was brought from Lourdes, in vain. Sister Angélique whispered that I should be the one taken there, to the black city of broken angels, that a fever like this one was not normal, that a fever like this was the work of the devil.

The public prosecutor did not follow up on the report.

Voices spoke to me, in long sine waves. I was tuned to every radio in the universe. For eleven days, I was no longer an orphan. My mother wrung out a cloth and placed it on my forehead. My father forced me to swallow bitter potions, *it's for your own good, Rothenberg gave us the recipe, an old secret from the Venice ghetto.* Several times I saw Momo writhing on the bed next to mine in the infirmary, during the day as well as at night. When he wasn't busy with his epileptic rodeos, he would stare at me, his cuddly donkey in his arms, with what remained of his strength. With what remained of mine, I would look away. If reality was Momo, I preferred my fever with its muffled waves, its numbed pangs, its dark tremors. I preferred to burn in the pure fire of my visions.

The antibiotics didn't work. I could have told them that. I could have told them that what I had could not be cured by penicillin or poultices, nor by the exorcism prayers secretly read out at night by Sister Angélique from a little book that resembled my callisthenics manual. The real problem was the tears.

I have done my best to avoid this subject. But we are going to have to talk about the tears. I had not shed any at all since the accident, since my family had been fused with metal in that crucible of fire. The psychologist said softly that I just hadn't *found* them yet. It wasn't for want of looking, though. No matter how I tried – picturing my parents' coffins, thinking about the unbearable coffin neatly arranged between them on the day of the funeral, about the wood that separated them when they should have been touching – still nothing came. But the world demanded my non-existent tears, and that unpaid debt was at the root of the disease tormenting my body.

At the age of sixteen years and eleven days, I opened my eyes in the middle of the night. Momo was sitting on the edge of my bed. He was tightly gripping my hand, and he was weeping. He was weeping like nobody has wept since then, he was weeping like someone at the foot of a cross, face thrown back, in the arms of the Madonna. He was weeping empires. He was weeping for me, because I couldn't.

In the morning, Sister Angélique declared it was a miracle. My fever had gone. She made me go outside, kneel under a conventicle of fading stars, and recite three Our Fathers. Souzix was already down in the courtyard, pacing around, shivering, a Cape of Piss draped over his shoulders.

From that day on, the kid with the Oran eyes, the sea urchin fisherman of few words, Momo and I were joined for life, bound in friendship until death. He was my tears, and I became his voice.

Blue, yellow, green.

Van Gogh's *The Starry Night*. A striking reproduction, almost indistinguishable from the real thing, was hung above Rothenberg's piano. I knew every detail of that picture because I spent so long staring at it. The day I used the word 'fake', Rothenberg slapped the back of my head.

'What if I play this?'

He crushed the opening chords of the 'Hammerklavier'.

'If I play this, is it fake, cretin? Are you saying it's not by Ludwig?'

'Calm down, Alon,' said his wife as she passed through the living room. 'You'll make yourself sick.'

'Do not mix up copy and interpretation, idiot. If this painting was a mere copy, I would have thrown it away long ago. What you see there is Van Gogh.'

'But he didn't paint it.'

'Who knows? Maybe he painted two versions. And even if he only painted one, this one would not exist if he hadn't painted the first. So you could say that he painted both. Or, more simply, that Van Gogh didn't paint this picture, but he did paint it all the same.'

'So when I play Beethoven ...'

'When *you* play Beethoven, Ludwig turns in his grave. But when Kempff plays Beethoven, when Fischer or that Argentine kid, Barenboim, plays Beethoven, that is something else altogether. When *they* play, it might not be Beethoven who is playing, but it is Beethoven who's playing all the same.'

Blue, yellow, green.

We are far from the train station where we met, you and I. Far from airports and public pianos. You are starting to regret asking me your favourite question, 'What is a man like you doing in a place like this?' But if you think I have strayed from the point, if you think I have lost the thread of my story with all this stuff about aeroplanes, deaf gods, orphans, paintings and, soon, girls named after flowers, it's because you are looking at it from too close up. You are furiously squinting and you are seeing the same thing I saw, fifty years ago.

Blue, yellow, green.

You do not realise that you are looking at *The Starry Night* with your nose practically touching the canvas. So, be patient. Let me distil the colours of my night.

When I turned up at the first PE lesson, a ghost freshly discharged from the infirmary, Rachid simply pointed to the bench.

'Not you,' he said while the others started running around the courtyard.

I sat next to Momo, whom nobody had ever tried to educate, not even physically. Rachid watched his students for a moment, clapping his hands and yelling: 'Let's go, let's go,' in his singsong voice, although those chants of '*Allons-y, allons-y*' produced no effect. Rachid did not take offence. He knew he was teaching a class of Titans condemned, for having insulted the gods, to carry the world on their shoulders. It would be too much to expect them to run fast as well.

The only one who made any real effort was Weasel. He went from one group to another, slowing down to let them catch him, then speeding off again. Most people did ten laps; he did fifteen. This was his trafficking time. He collected money, promises, requests, put them on an already virtual market for which he was the central calculator; he sold, bought, increased prices, auctioned off chores, knick-knacks, coloured inks, chocolate bars, small change and paper money. Weasel remembered everything. No physical exchanges were made in the courtyard, not with Toad hopping about suspiciously around the edges. The transactions would not be carried out until later, in a ballet of brushing, intersecting hands that passed and palmed currencies and commodities in corridors and queues, under desks and tables, a discreet underground network apparently unconnected to the blameless faces floating around at the surface.

Between two 'Let's go's, Rachid came over and stared at me, frowning.

'I heard you tried to run away. That they found you eight kilometres from here after an hour. I was very disappointed when they told me that.'

He put a foot on the bench, very close to me, and bent down to tie his laces.

'Eight kilometres per hour,' he murmured. 'If you want to get out of here, you'll have to run faster than that.'

The priest had not said anything. He had seen me at breakfast but had not mentioned my little escapade. He had even *smiled* at me. But when Toad whistled for the end of the PE lesson, the first-floor window opened. Sénac's eyes met mine and he slowly nodded.

He was waiting for me, still standing in front of the window, eye glued to his telescope. He pointed out three black marks drifting through the sky, floating on an updraught.

'The little bearded vulture is learning to fly. It's the first time its parents have gone this far from the nest. I've been watching them for a year. They nest under the ledge above Les Confins. Magnificent, aren't they? Did you know that there are only a few pairs left in the whole of the Pyrenees? It's an endangered species. Very fragile. They abandon their nest at the slightest disturbance.'

He put down his telescope, went back to his desk and clasped his fingers under his chin, under that strange baby-like face where only the eyes appeared old. The rest was pink, engorged, glowing with health. Sénac never had a hair out of place and his cheeks were always impeccably shaved, the skin burned by the fire of the razor blade and sanctified with a halo of cologne.

'I have prayed for you, Joseph. Many times, I have asked God to show me where I went wrong. To show me what I had done to deserve a telephone call from the gendarmerie, for the name of Les Confins to be publicly sullied by you running away.'

'It wasn't you.'

'I beg your pardon?'

'It wasn't you, Monsieur l'abbé. It was Toa— Monsieur Marthod.'

'Ah yes, that ludicrous story. He doesn't show it, but I know that Monsieur Marthod was very hurt by your lie. Thankfully, the gendarmes are not that gullible.'

'He attacked me, to get his revenge!'

'Revenge? For what? Why was he angry with you?'

Because I lied about my black eye. I didn't slip in the showers that you made him scrub.

'Joseph?'

'I don't know ...'

'You *saw* Monsieur Marthod that night? Saw him like I can see you now?'

'No.'

'So, let's go over this. You have no injuries. You didn't *see* Monsieur Marthod. And he had no reason to want revenge. Is that correct?'

'Yes. Yes, Monsieur l'abbé.'

'Isn't it possible that you imagined the whole thing? You were extremely feverish.'

'I ... I don't know.'

Sénac took a long breath. His hands resting – no, pressing down – on the desk in front of him were shaking slightly.

'It's a simple question. Is it possible that you imagined the whole thing? *Yes or no?*'

'Yes.'

'There you go. You imagined it all. I'm glad you admit it.'

His hands relaxed, then smoothed down his neatly ironed cassock.

'Were it not for my good relations with the authorities, it could have been very embarrassing. What if there had been an investigation? Did you think about that? For many of your classmates, we are the only family they have ever known. What would become of them if Les Confins was closed? There is nothing out there for them, you understand?'

'Yes, Monsieur l'abbé.'

'I wasn't wrong to put my trust in you, was I?'

'No, Monsieur l'abbé.'

'I hope you are right. Because you wouldn't be the first boy to disappoint me.'

'Like Danny?'

I don't know why I mentioned that name. The priest instantly stiffened.

'Who told you about Danny?'

'The others.'

'And what did they say?'

'That he was dead.'

'Don't be ridiculous. Danny isn't dead. He will return in glory, the day his sins are forgiven, and Christ will walk with him. Go and join the others now. I have an announcement to make.'

The announcement concerned a visit from a very important person, one of the diocese's biggest donors, a man whose continued generosity was essential for the future functioning of Les Confins. The priest never actually made this announcement: the visitor in question was already there, standing in the middle of the entrance hall, when we went downstairs. He had arrived early, thanks to the Triumph GT6 parked in the courtyard and almost impossible to see through the cluster of orphans that surrounded it. I saw Father Sénac look embarrassed for the first time in my life. And the last time too.

'Monsieur le comte, I wasn't expecting you so early. Nobody told me ...'

The rhythm was about to enter my life. The rhythm of Rothenberg, Beethoven, the Stones. The rhythm of the devil – and of God, because rhythm is the only thing those two share. The count had something extraordinary, and it wasn't his height or his elegance, nor even the fact that he was wearing the very Oxford shoes from which my dead family had made its fortune. The extraordinary thing was sitting in the passenger seat of his car, and when the car door opened I realised that it wasn't the curves of the Triumph six-cylinder that the boys had been admiring. A girl got out. Or, rather, a young woman, even if she wasn't much older than me. She looked uncomfortable, and who can blame her? Eighty-four eyes were staring at her, transfixed, five-year-olds and seventeen-year-olds and everything in between projecting upon her their fantasies of mothers and lovers and disturbing mixtures of the two. Weasel was pretending not to have noticed her; Sinatra was practically ogling her, so hard was he trying to resemble his father. Edison, the only boy who was genuinely interested in the car, stuck his head inside.

Souzix touched our extraordinary visitor with his fingertip. Startled, she tried to sidestep him, but he grabbed a handful of her dress so he could feel the softness of the fabric, then rubbed his forehead against it. Souzix was, in his way, a connoisseur – this girl was not wearing just any old dress. It was a Dior. Maman had taken me into the shop on Rue Montaigne so often that the salesgirls there considered me a member of their family. I used to wander around the atelier while she tried on the latest creations, and I learned quite a few things during those visits. This red dress with its flared skirt, fastened by a large button on the shoulder, had been designed by Marc Bohan for the 1961–62 haute-couture collection. She must have borrowed it from her mother. The count was rich, but not a spendthrift.

'Have you seen *Mary Poppins*?' Souzix asked the girl.

She examined him, horrified.

'So … have you seen it or not?'

'Yes … Papa, are we going inside?'

'Come here, Rose. Father, allow me to introduce my daughter.'

The rose approached, walking stiffly between two rows of orphans. She gave an outmoded curtsey to the priest.

'I didn't know you would get here so quickly, Monsieur le comte. Mademoiselle, would you like some refreshment?'

'For my part, I would like to see this new roof that it was so important to have built, and the cost of which meant that my wife could not buy a new car this year,' the count said, laughing. 'But what can we do? Our dear children must be protected from the rain, mustn't they?'

'They are all very grateful to you, Monsieur le comte. If you would follow me, I—'

'I think my daughter can be spared this visit. She is tired from the journey. Could she rest somewhere while we look around?'

The priest met my eyes which had, a second earlier, been riveted on the delicate curves of the flower.

'Joseph, please show our guest to my office, and ask Sister Albertine to bring her whatever she would like to drink.'

'A Coca-Cola,' the girl said.

Forty-two boys guffawed. Sinatra shouted: 'We're all out – there's only champagne left!' The rose gritted her teeth, the priest loudly clapped his hands, and the troop stood to attention. Toad collared Sinatra, who was standing in the back row, and frogmarched him into the building. One hand on the back of his neck, like a pair of old friends. Sinatra's feet barely even touched the ground.

I led the girl up to the first floor and stood aside to let her enter the office. She looked surprised. She paced around the room, glancing about disdainfully, eyes ablaze under her black fringe. She was tall and very pale, as if the blood from her cheeks had all drained down into her dress. She had a very forceful, almost masculine nose. Her teeth were on the large side, good for biting into apples, and the corners of her eyes hardly drooped at all. I had no idea she was beautiful, or about to be. She stopped in front of the bookshelves, her finger on the spine of a large book stuck between two statues of the Virgin.

'That's bizarre, isn't it?' She pronounced it *bizaarre*, lengthening her As elegantly. She didn't lengthen any other vowels, though, because that would not have been elegant.

'What's bizarre?' I asked, my A deplorably banal.

'This encyclopaedia. There's only one volume, T–Z. Why?'

'I don't know. It's Sén— I mean, the book belongs to Monsieur l'abbé.'

'Hmm. It's true that encyclopaedias are expensive. I have the *Britannica*. Complete.'

'And you read it while drinking Coca-Cola ...'

She gave me a long, cold look, the kind that women bestow when they are declaring war. War without mercy. Then she began pacing again, stopping this time by the piano and running a finger along the lid.

'You shouldn't touch anything,' I murmured.

'Turn the light on.'

'Huh?'

'I said turn the light on.'

I did as I was told. She gestured with her chin at the fluorescent ceiling lamp.

'You see that? My father paid for that. He donated fifteen thousand francs to have the entire electrical system refurbished three years ago. I remember it well: I couldn't get what I wanted for my birthday that year, because we had to *give to the orphans*. If it wasn't for him, you'd all be albinos, forced to live in the dark like rats. And you'd be constantly wet from the rain because the roof used to leak until we gave you the money to have it repaired. So there you go – you'd be wet albino rats. So I'll touch anything

I want. Because all of this,' she concluded, spreading her arms out wide, 'is ours.'

She opened the lid of the piano. *Her* piano. Her hands were even paler than her face, like the hands of a marble statue. She had the most beautiful fingers I had ever seen. And when she played, I held my breath. Not because she was talented – she wasn't. But she played Beethoven, Sonata no. 26, 'Les Adieux'. A clumsy, hesitant Beethoven, a panic-stricken Beethoven, groping around in the bushes of deafness. She caught sight of me and frowned.

'Why are you looking at me like that?'

'No reason.'

'Haven't you ever seen anyone play the piano before? No, of course not. In a place like this, you're probably more used to hearing banjos.'

'You're not supposed to play it like that.'

'Not supposed to play *what* like that?'

I walked over slowly, each footstep crushing the promise I had made to the priest not to touch his piano, and by the time I placed my fingers on the keyboard the promise was dead. Rose was still sitting on the stool. I stood beside her, touching the keys without pressing down on them, paralysed by the weight of expectation.

'So?' she jeered.

She smelled of powder, marigold, lavender. Something medicinal too. And the top note of her fragrance was that indefinable touch of arrogance, a beautiful, nocturnal, aristocratic arrogance that flees the impertinence of the sun. She smelled of the moon. I could hear her fragile heart beating. I could not cover up that heartbeat – that would have been criminal – but I had to put the force of the 'Adieux' into those first chords. I had to play quickly, before someone found us. I had to play slowly, because one cannot say goodbye without some hesitation, without turning around several times, as when Momo, salty-lipped, had seen his land sinking into the mist behind him. I had to fit all of this into a restricted, non-existent volume, barely a few cubic centimetres under my ten fingers, the Presto the Adagio the fury the silence, under my palms curled around imaginary oranges.

I put all of that into three simple pressures. *E flat G*. Rose jumped. *B flat F*. She gaped at me. *C minor*. 'Les Adieux'. The door closed, softly, on a place to which we would not return. Rose had started to tremble. Her breathing was strange, almost whistling. Between the notes, she sensed sad Caravelles, moments of incandescence, Ludwig's ghosts and mine too. Those intervals also contained things that neither Ludwig nor I had seen. Wars, reconciliations, promises not to recommence, recommencements. There was a kiss in a garden full of olive trees, thirty pieces of silver in the moonlight, there was a torn curtain, a blinding peace, a centurion who realised he had made a mistake. There was a feeling of dread, and in the cracks of that dread, beauty was already blossoming. Staggering, Rose held on to the corner of the piano. After twenty or so bars, I lifted my hands. Those were the first bars of music I had played in my life.

'Tremendous.'

The count stood in the doorway, applauding with the refinement of a regular concertgoer. The priest stood behind him and he was applauding too, with exaggerated slowness. The right corner of his mouth twitched upwards, a dissonant anomaly next to those smooth, round cheeks. His entire being braced itself against that smile, the smile of a clown without make-up.

'Tremendous,' repeated the count. 'It was magnificent, wasn't it, Rose?'

Rose looked in turn at the piano, at me, at the piano again. She could not understand. Could not understand how this puny little boy who did not even fully inhabit his own skin could have produced *that*. I couldn't understand it either.

'Joseph is one of our best students,' the priest announced.

'Now, Joseph, if you would leave us? And come back to see me in an hour … There's something I'd like to discuss with you.'

'Just a minute, Father, just a minute … My daughter needs piano lessons. Could Joseph teach her, perhaps?'

'It would be a pleasure, but Joseph already has a great deal of work and I fear he could not find the time before you return to Paris.'

'We are not returning to Paris. Or rather, Rose and her mother are not returning to Paris. They will stay at our property here at least until the start of next year, enough time to settle certain unimportant matters. I will come back here for the weekend every two weeks.'

Sénac's smile did not waver.

'I see, I see. Or rather, I don't entirely see. Rose is … sixteen, I believe? She must be starting the lower sixth, no? At Louis-le-Grand, you told me. I am afraid that the academic level at the school in Lourdes—'

'Rose will be home-schooled,' the count interrupted. 'Naturally, I attach great importance to the quality of her education. And to her piano lessons, because she won't be able to return to the conservatoire until March or April. I will send my chauffeur here every Saturday, and he will bring Joseph back just after the lesson. About three in the afternoon, if that works for you?'

'Take lessons with *him*?' Rose exploded. 'But he's …'

The priest and the count waited. Neither of them had understood what she meant. He's *an orphan*.

'He's what?'

'He's … He must be busy.'

'I'm sure he will find the time. So, is that settled?'

'Absolutely, Monsieur le comte.'

'Excellent, excellent. Thank you, Father, for your hospitality. I will come back another time to have a longer talk about the next investments necessary for the well-being of our flock. Are you coming, darling?'

His daughter made an enormous effort to detach herself from the piano, regather what remained of her strength and fire a look of pure hate in my direction, as if all of this were my fault. She was a mediocre musician. I had thrown that mediocrity in her face, and for a long time I thought she was angry with me for that. Later, I realised that she envied me my freedom. It was still a clumsy, fledgling freedom, a pile of downy feathers that had to flap its wings frantically to keep from crashing, but which, in the space of twenty bars, had soared like the royal eagle it would one day become.

Rose smiled when she passed me – her father had taught her good manners. The hate she felt for me was the first secret we would share, a solid foundation on which we would build all the rest: walls of contempt, turrets of indifference, machicolations of disdain, posterns of pettiness, counterscarps of suppressed anger, a fortress of resentment and bitterness that would crumble six months later at the first breath of wind, proof that it was not so solid after all.

'Sit down and type.'

At the priest's request, I had come back upstairs after dinner. He was deep in his Bible when I entered. He pointed at the Hermès 3000 without glancing up. I was a virtuoso typist by now. Paper, roller, lever. Insert, turn, shift. The Hermès 3000 was ready.

'"For the attention of the Departmental Director." Next line. "Following your request for an assessment of Joseph Marty with regard to his placement with a host family, I regret to inform you that the young man's psychological instability" ... Why aren't you typing?'

I had stopped at 'host family'.

'TYPE!' yelled the priest.

He was white-faced. Almost immediately, he raised his hand in apology.

'All right … Where were we? … Ah, yes: "the young man's psychological instability, combined with a tendency to lie, forces me, to my great regret, to give you an unfavourable response." Next line, just put the usual sign-off. Secular, though. This is for management.'

The letters danced before my eyes. I had the most awful stomach ache.

'Is something wrong, Joseph?'

'You're not letting me leave …'

'I'm letting you stay. For your own good. And also for the good of the family in question.'

He picked up a document and placed a pair of glasses on the end of his nose.

'The … Desmarets.'

'Our neighbours?'

The Desmarets lived opposite us. They were both tiny. They were retirees, and whenever they were asked: '*Retraités de quoi?*', meaning what job had they retired from, they would invariably reply: '*Retraités de petite taille*' – small retirees – a joke that made them laugh very loudly and got on our nerves, even if, deep down, we liked them. They had never had any children, only that red cat which Henri had almost killed with his father's rifle. And they had offered to adopt me. To look after me. Worthless me.

'It's only temporary, Joseph. They could make another request in six months and I would reassess it then.'

'It's disgusting.'

Sénac leaned forward. He was breathing normally. Even today, I couldn't swear that I had heard him yelling. Perhaps he whispered 'Type,' in his usual soft voice. But for me, everything was yelling.

'What is "disgusting", Joseph?'

'You're punishing me.'

'I don't like that word. "Punishment" suggests vengeance. I prefer "correction" because it suggests the hope of change, like correcting a trajectory. You ran away. Surely you didn't imagine I would let that pass without comment? And after running away, after looking in my eyes and promising me that you deserved to be given a second chance, you played the piano.'

'Only to help that girl.'

'To help her, or to show off how well you can play? To help her, or for the pleasure of doing something forbidden? I advised you on your first day to beware your pride. I have known many young men like you, from good families, who came to an orphanage quite late and believed they could get away with anything because they would leave soon anyway, because they had friends in high places.'

'I swear I will never touch your piano again. I didn't know it meant so much to you.'

'It's not *my* piano – it was here when I took over from Father Puig. It's a piano, that's all. I don't even play it. But for you, that instrument represents temptation, your life before. And that life is over. Here, at Les Confins, we are preparing your future.'

'You're not my father!'

I had shouted. Sénac nodded. I believe he had waited a long time for this moment.

'You're wrong, Joseph. I *am* your father. See? You address me as "Father" every day, but you don't believe it. I am your father, first of all, because of the power vested in me by the State. I am your father, above all, by grace of the mission given to the Apostles, two thousand years ago, by Our Lord Jesus Christ. Like him, I understand your distress. Like him, I will destroy the temple and raise it up again. My role is not to please you. My role is to raise you up.'

He walked around the desk.

'Kneel, because you are a sinner.'

'I thought you wanted to raise me up.'

He grabbed me by the back of my neck. He was not very tall and he was quite old, but he was incredibly strong.

'Together let us ask the Lord to light our way by confessing our sins. *Confíteor Deo omnipotenti ...*'

My knees hit the flagstones. I sought within myself for the protection of that anger which had so often saved me. In vain. I was full of vast blank echoes.

'*Mea culpa,*' Sénac whispered. '*Mea culpa, mea maxima culpa ...*'

He pressed down on my skull with all his strength, lowering my sinner's eyes to the ground, to my clasped fingers. It was then, staring at my hands, that I saw it. The sign that even now enables me to spot an orphan in a crowd, at night. To recognise a brother at a single glance, from among the multitude. It's a simple detail.

'... *et dimissis peccatis nostris, perducat nos ad vitam æternam.* Amen. You will not go to bed until you have finished my letters.'

It's a simple detail. A very small thing.

All orphans have hands that shake.

When midnight came, I was still typing, my fingers throbbing from *sincere gratitude*s and *brother in Christ*s.

I don't believe in miracles, but sometimes you have no choice but to face the truth. Around one in the morning, I took a break. While I was stretching, my eyes fell on the encyclopaedia volume that had been left there, another orphan, beside a book on ornithology.

The miracle is not that I took the volume. Souzix had asked me about the identity of the Thérèse to whom Beethoven had dedicated his twenty-fourth sonata, and I thought I might find the answer here. I looked up and down the corridor – there was no one around. The book was heavy. I can still feel its weight.

It's crazy to think how much life weighs between T and Z. There were loads of Thérèses in there. Thérèse of Lisieux, Teresa d'Avila … Apparently it was a name prone to saintliness. None of them had known Beethoven; they were all born too soon, or too late. And, in all honesty, none of them looked like music lovers (the encyclopaedia was illustrated).

I heard a footstep. In a panic, I tried to put the volume away. But my hands, stiff from hours of typing, had stopped obeying me. Instead of sliding neatly into place, the book hit the edge of the shelf and fell, its leather wings outspread, pages to the floor. Paralysed with fear, I waited. Nobody came in. The footsteps faded to silence. Maybe just Toad, on his nightly patrol. Or a nun, racked by doubt, on her way to the church where the cold would kill it. I waited for a long time before I finally dared to move. At last, I picked up the book.

It had fallen open at random.

If you believe in randomness, that is, which is not something I have been able to claim since that night.

There are days when I feel tired. When my fingers are heavy, when I don't want to play any more. When I think: 'What's the point? She's not going to come.' And I feel like a coward. Because others before me have felt it too, this fatigue, in jazz clubs where a howl of brass has pushed back the dawn, in Paris, Chicago, Johannesburg, in dive bars, in townships, in vaults, in old churches where even the dead shiver with cold, piano fingers, trumpet fingers, violin-organ-double-bass-saxophone fingers, white fingers, black fingers, thousands of fingers that forged music to undo the silence.

On days like that, I think about The Lookout and my hands become beautiful again, filled with youth and ardour. I am a member of a secret society, a society so secret that even at its height it had only seven members. I am not talking about those childish conspiracies, those little gangs invented as a game. The Lookout saved men who were not quite, not yet men.

'Didn't you get enough last time?'

It was 10 August 1969, and Sinatra raised his fists in warning as I lifted up the trapdoor that led to the roof. Edison, Souzix, Weasel and Sinatra were sitting in a circle around their homemade transistor radio. Weasel instantly turned it off, but I had time to hear a voice. A voice I would later learn to know, the voice of an enchantment that came from out of the mountains to put a spell on the valleys. I would learn that even an angel could speak with a Spanish accent.

Their eight eyes widened even further when Momo emerged behind me.

'We want to be members of The Lookout.'

'Request denied,' said Weasel, who gave a signal to Sinatra. Go ahead, give them a good kicking, knock some sense into them.

Sinatra came over and stopped dead when he saw that I wasn't moving. He had been in enough fights to know that this was the calmness of an armed man. He was right. I put my hand in my pocket. He tensed, expecting the gleam of a knife blade. I took out a sheet of paper.

'It's a page from the priest's encyclopaedia. If he realises I've cut it out, he'll kill me.'

Weasel shrugged.

'We don't have any vacancies. A page from a dictionary isn't going to change that.'

'It's not any old page from a dictionary. It's the most important page of all. The only one you have to know in the entire encyclopaedia.'

I carefully unfolded the paper. Trying to look relaxed, although my fingers were trembling. You can't handle a bomb like that without sweating a little bit. Four faces froze. Almost the same effect that I create, now, when playing Beethoven.

The page began with VULPIN: *annual grass of the Poaceae family*. Suffice to say these lads did not give a shit about grass. They were staring at the next word down. VULVA. And, below it, the immense black-and-white illustration, a quarter of a page all to itself, a quarter of a page dedicated to the cartography of that terra incognita and its astonishing reliefs, itemised in exotic italics: *Mons Veneris*, *Clitoris*, *Inner and Outer Labia*. The drawing was admirably precise: you could see part of the spread thighs, you could imagine the artist lying there, notebook in hand, only a few centimetres from his model, so close that you were left to wonder how he had not been burned, blinded, driven mad by such intimacy, how he had found the strength to sketch each hair, to give that graceful fold to the right lip, slightly more open than the left.

Edison ogled the page open-mouthed, fascinated by this futuristic mechanism with its invisible nuts and bolts. Sinatra gave a sarcastic, contemptuous smile – *you really think I've never seen one of those before?* – which was somewhat belied by the bulge in his shorts. Weasel's eyes flickered from the drawing to me. Souzix asked: 'Is it a bear?'

'It's a girl, you idiot.'

Souzix took the page from my hands. Edison tried to grab it from him and Sinatra stepped between them. I calmly raised my hand.

'Everyone can take a turn.'

They stared at me with stupefaction, and with the admiration owed to someone who can keep his cool in the middle of an earthquake. My composure was hard-earned. I had drunk in every detail of the drawing the night before until I was sated, until I was used to it – not yet aware that this was the kind of thing you don't get used to.

'If you let me and Momo become members of The Lookout, the page is yours. *Ours*. If not ...'

'If not?'

'It's too dangerous to keep it on my own. What if the priest found it? I'd have to burn it.'

All four of them turned pale.

'You wouldn't dare,' said Sinatra.

'No? Well, for starters, I'm going to tear it in two.'

I lifted up the page, held the top of it between the index finger and thumb of each hand, and ...

'Stop!' shouted Weasel. 'Okay, okay, you can join. But not the moron.'

'His name is Momo. Call him a moron one more time and I'll smash your face in.'

I was serious, and he knew it. Momo smiled. Momo always smiled.

'All right, calm down. I vote in favour. Lads?'

'Me too,' said Edison.

Souzix nodded solemnly. Only Sinatra remained defiant.

'How do we know he's not trying to trick us? Maybe Sénac's using him to spy on us?'

'If Sénac knew we were here, he wouldn't just spy on us.'

'Do what you want then,' said Sinatra. 'But if he turns out to be a traitor, don't say I didn't warn you.'

'All right, so that's four votes in favour.'

Weasel held out his hand to me and then, after a brief hesitation, to Momo.

'Welcome to The Lookout.'

I am often asked if I would *really* have torn that page. Of course I wouldn't, but not for the reasons you imagine, even if a teenager's blood beats a little harder than any adult's. I thought about the woman who modelled for the picture. It can't have been easy, showing herself like that, opening herself up for our edification. It took courage. That woman lived somewhere; as we were admiring her, she was probably busy getting ready for the day, making coffee in her dressing gown. Perhaps she was old and the drawing had been done many years before. Perhaps she, too, looked at the encyclopaedia, at her young vulva, with a sigh of melancholy. So, no, I wasn't going to tear it. I did not wish to disrespect a heroine.

'One last point,' added Weasel. 'Here, it's every man for himself. If something happens to you, we don't know you. If something happens to us, you don't know us. Repeat it back to me.'

'Every man for himself.'

'Perfect. Now, keep your mouth shut. Both of you. Thanks to you, we missed half of Marie-Ange.'

Marie-Ange Roig. I made her acquaintance that night, when they turned the radio back on. The ideal woman that each of us constructed was a collage, a clumsy assemblage of fragments of beauty glimpsed here and there. When Camille bent down in her baggy vest to pick up her son. On the cover of a magazine during an outing to the village, or through the window of the bus taking us to Lourdes in the summer as a convertible overtook us. We could debate it endlessly, say that the perfect woman should have a figure like Gina Lollobrigida or Sophia Loren, a smile like Claudia Cardinale or Grace Kelly, eyes like Bardot or Marie Laforêt. But when it came to the voice, we were all in agreement. She had to speak like Marie-Ange Roig. Admittedly the lack of any competition offered her a somewhat unfair advantage.

Marie-Ange presented the show *Crossroads of the Night*, to which the members of The Lookout listened religiously every Sunday evening. It was broadcast on Sud Radio, the only station that Edison's homemade radio could pick up. Her voice rose from Andorra towards the Pic Blanc. From there, it mounted a medium wave of 367 metres (the jingles kept repeating this, it must have been important) and, riding that wave, attacked the summits, braving the cold, the solitude, the storms, until it reached us – we never imagined that she might be talking to anyone else. Sometimes during a storm her voice would be lost, unseated, its mount struck dead by lightning. When that happened, we feared we would never hear her again. But the voice was eternal. I like to think, fifty years later, that its scattered echoes are still travelling, at the speed of sound, towards the unreachable edges of the cosmos. That, one day, a distant and infinite intelligence will receive its signal. And listen to it, thoughtfully. And conclude that while we may have been stupid, at least we were beautiful.

Marie-Ange vanished from the airwaves an hour later, leaving us in the middle of a night that was just a little darker, a little colder.

Those hollows between the shadows were the most dangerous.

'Shall we play a game?' I suggested.

'Poker? We don't have any money.'

'We don't need money.'

'How can you play poker without money?'

'I never mentioned poker!'

'You said you wanted to play, didn't you?'

'Maybe he's thinking of blackjack,' Sinatra said. 'But you need cash for that too.'

'Stop talking about cash! I just mean a game. For the pleasure of it.'

'For the *pleasure*?'

They didn't understand. A gulf still separated us, even if I had just become a professional orphan.

'We don't know any games that are played for pleasure.'

'We can just invent one.'

They exchanged a look. Those four spent their lives looking at one another so they wouldn't fall, like a kid turning around to make sure Papa had not let go of the bike without telling him, after taking off the stabilisers and swearing he would keep hold.

'We could do ... a sadness contest,' suggested Edison, stimulated by the word 'invent'.

'What's a sadness contest?'

'The winner is the one who tells the saddest story. And the prize is he gets each of the others to do one of his chores for him.'

'Except cleaning the toilets,' said Sinatra. 'I'm not doing that twice.'

'And Momo is excused,' I added.

'I'll start,' Edison announced.

The sun was rising over the Senegal river. In the local café where she worked as a waitress, Edison's mother had fallen in love with a handsome gentleman in a suit, a French diplomat who invited her to go with him to France, in the Jura, to the United

Nations office where he worked. Nobody had told this sixteen-year-old girl from the suburbs of Saint-Louis that there was no United Nations office in the Jura. The diplomat actually ran a transport company, which wasn't bad anyway. He kept her in a small apartment above a bar where he would visit her regularly, and where he would sometimes send his friends to help make ends meet. Edison was born, the father more or less unknown, though he was definitely a white man. One night, the diplomat invited her to a sophisticated party, and when the beautiful girl from Saint-Louis, feeling a little tired, asked him what a sophisticated party was, he explained: 'A place where people will appreciate that pretty chocolate-coloured skin,' and he slapped her bottom. Edison never knew if his mother's pretty chocolate-coloured skin had been appreciated or not, because she and the diplomat were killed on their way back. The diplomat had two grams of cheap champagne in his bloodstream. Ironically, he crashed their car into one of his own trucks, which had broken down earlier that evening by the side of the departmental road at the entrance to the city.

The others applauded and turned towards me. I wanted to tell them about the aeroplane – I saw the man in his too-large jacket, scared away by the Fourniers' rifle, his heartrending gouache and his misshapen Christ – I opened my mouth but no sound came out and in the end two idiotic tears rolled from the corners of my eyes. They all looked away.

'You're out,' declared Weasel calmly. 'My turn.'

He entered the competition with the collapse of the apartment building that had cost his parents their lives. Then he raised the stakes by describing the world that fell on top of him through his CinemaScope view from under the bed: it was a real disaster movie, a *Titanic* of cracked concrete and plaster built by slumlords, an avalanche of dust and screams and then silence, as if the building had finally fallen asleep, even the shoemaker on the ground floor who usually worked all night long. The last pair of shoes he re-soled were found intact, and their owners dropped the money they owed him onto his coffin. Weasel was inventing certain details, without a doubt, but his audience considered it a mark of respect and again applauded warmly.

Sinatra described the tearful farewell scene between his mother and Ol' Blue Eyes. The shopkeeper from Figeac wrote to the famous crooner soon afterwards to inform him that she was pregnant. Frank wrote back to say he was on his way. He did not make it back to France because the pregnant mother was interned before he could come, and the singer's Jewish agent would not have allowed it anyway.

'Why his *Jewish* agent?' I asked.

'I don't know – he's Jewish, that's all. Why, what's your problem? Are *you* Jewish?'

'No. Well, a bit. My grandfather was Jewish. I'm a quarter Jewish, sort of.'

'It doesn't work like that with the Jews. You either are or you're not. Anyway, if it's just a quarter, that's, what, fifteen, twenty per cent? That's not too bad.'

'Well, it's definitely better than being a hundred per cent stupid.'

Sinatra squinted suspiciously and I gave him my best smile. Edison tried not to laugh.

'Yeah, definitely,' he finally agreed.

There was weak applause for Sinatra. Everyone turned to look at Souzix.

He shrugged. 'I don't have a sad story.'

'You're kidding!' said Weasel. 'You must know one, surely?'

'Nope.'

'Just make one up. I mean, you're always going on about *Mary Poppins* ... Isn't that a sad story?'

'I don't know.'

'How can you not know?'

'Well, I haven't seen the whole film. My adoptive mother and her new boyfriend took me to the cinema, but they had a fight at the beginning of the film. Jean-Pierre said that Suzanne was a slut so she stormed out, and when she came back Mary Poppins and her friends had just jumped into a cartoon, and Suzanne had brought the rifle with her, and Jean-Pierre yelled, and she fired the gun, and there was blood everywhere and they had to stop the film, and then the police came, and that's how Jean-Pierre ended up in the cemetery and Suzanne in prison, and I never got to see the end of *Mary Poppins*, and I'd really like to find someone who's seen it so they can tell me what happens. So, no, sorry, I don't know any sad stories.'

A week later, I chopped wood for Souzix, Sinatra swept the courtyard, Weasel shined forty-two pairs of shoes, and Edison did the washing-up. Souzix said he obviously didn't understand the rules of our big-boy games.

The endless wait. It happened every Saturday, except one. Rose's house was as grand and solemn as Les Confins, more like a monastery than a family home. Black walls reared up at the end of a park whose paths intersected at right angles, overrun by plants that had grown wild from the greenhouses and flowerbeds after the death of their last gardener, the house's louvred shutters half hidden behind the leaves of giant palm trees. In winter, when night fell early, the place was alive with mad shadows. I quickened my pace, afraid that I would meet the devil at one of those junctions, wearing a trilby, pact in hand. *I will make you the greatest musician of all time. I will give you the gift of rhythm. Sign here.* In other places, on other crossroads, certain musicians had signed. Paganini, the greatest violinist of all time, of whom it was said that his mother had sold his soul when he was born. The blues guitarist Robert Johnson, a mediocre musician who became a virtuoso after vanishing for weeks near Clarksdale, Mississippi. At the intersection of Route 49 and Route 61, went the legend, the devil had tuned his guitar. And maybe Rothenberg too, for all I knew, during his travels in Poland. Except that Rothenberg, like Paganini, had been forced to sign the pact. Not by his mother, but by men in neatly ironed uniforms.

Toad had taken me to the manor house for that first lesson – Sénac had insisted, declining the count's offer to send his chauffeur – in the old DS that the French government had generously offered to Les Confins. It was supposedly the former official vehicle of a senator or secretary of state. There were some suspicious brown stains on the back seat. Every time one of the nuns sat down there, we laughed as they pressed themselves against the door, worried that the stains had been made by diabolical fluids.

Toad had watched me from the corner of his eye throughout the drive, with a little smile on his face. He spoke only once, when he put his hand on the knob for the radio.

'Apparently you like music?'

'Yes ...'

'Me too.'

He took his hand away from the radio and began to sing: *'Against the Viet Minh, against the enemy, wherever duty beckons, soldier of France ...'*

He tapped me on the shoulder while he was driving.

'Come on, sing! You're not going to go crying to the gendarmes because I made you sing, are you?'

'I don't know the words ...'

'Oh Legionnaire, the battle that begins ... fucking repeat it!'

'The battle that begins ...'

'Fill our souls with ardour and courage ...'

'Ardour and courage ...'

'That's good, son! *Let grenades and rubble rain down, our victory will burn more brightly.'*

And he repeated this while looking at me, driving blind along a part of the road where each curve had destroyed lives.

'Our victory will burn more brightly! You don't seem to like this song ... You have a problem with the army?'

'I don't know.'

'If there weren't men, good men, who sacrificed themselves for little shits like you, France would have ceased to exist long ago. We'd be speaking bloody Arabic or Vietna-fucking-mese. And you know who would be to blame? De Gaulle. But not only him. Coty, too. Mendès France. All those weak bastards. Is that what you like, weakness?'

'I don't know ...'

'"I don't know, I don't know ..." You know how to fucking whine, though, don't you? Are you a weak bastard too, eh? Hang on, at least tell me you're not queer ...'

His hand shot between my thighs and tightly gripped what it found there. Lights flashed before my eyes. My stomach turned. *Don't yell.* Toad whistled.

'Well, well, you're a big boy, aren't you?'

He squeezed harder.

'It'd be a shame if you didn't love the ladies, with a weapon like that.'

His hand lingered there a little longer, then he suddenly let go of me to jerk the steering wheel to the left. The DS just made it through the bend. 'Those fucking queers,' Toad muttered, shaking his head. After that, he didn't speak again.

He was sitting in the car now, smoking through the open window, while I waited in a dark corridor, on an oak bench hollowed out by years of thin Jansenist arses. Flowers were growing on the wall opposite me, an exotic jungle undetectable from outside. Indian reed, stapelia, China limodoron ... eighteenth-century colour engravings covered the wall from floor to ceiling. Some of the names were lost in the darkness. Every Saturday I would wait for an hour or more before being received by Rose, and I always imagined that it was for no reason. I was wrong – I did not wait for nothing – but I didn't know that until Saturday, 7 February 1970.

I am not obsessed by dates. It's just that I promised not to forget anything. And a 7 February is not a 12 March or an 8 April. The light is not the same. The flowers are not the same, except those that some patient engraver had embalmed in those big black frames.

After an hour, the governess showed me into a reception room. In a teal sweater and white trousers, Rose was languishing in front of a cheap Kawai, an old bar-room piano that clashed horribly with the ceiling frescoes of cherubs painted haphazardly on shores of plaster. She did not say hello, did not look at me. She simply moved along the bench, as far as possible, so that I could sit there beside her without the risk of contagion. Her mother came in, a small, frail woman who murmured simply: 'Oh, it's you, the orphan.' She said it without contempt, in the same tone as a nurse who was used to the stench of gangrene. She signalled to the governess to sit down in a corner of the room and then she left. The old lady chaperoned us during the whole hour that I was there, a completely pointless precaution given the visceral mutual dislike between Rose and myself. But things had started like that for Tristan and Isolde, and the family did not want to take the risk that one day an opera might be written about us.

Rose was pale, arrogant. Rose was as thin as an Indian reed, with the same utter lack of talent for music. I suddenly felt sorry for Rothenberg: perhaps I was his Rose? Despite the scratches inflicted on him by my thorny nature, my old teacher had put up with me for years, his only protest being the occasional slap to the back of my head. After thirty minutes, the governess fell asleep and began to snore. Rose raised her hands from the keyboard.

'That's enough. You should play it yourself. Just make a mistake now and then and they'll think it's me.'

Playing the piano was all I wanted to do. But I didn't want to get caught in this girl's trap. The air between us grew harder, as in those dark dreams in which I am running from the back of an aeroplane towards the cockpit where the pilot is making a bad choice. She picked up a book and ignored me. I played a few half-hearted chords. The first one to speak would kneel before the other. I had my pride.

'What does your father do?' I asked.

'He's in industry.'

'Why aren't you going back to Paris if you're supposed to be starting the lower sixth?'

'You're not being paid to ask questions.'

'I'm not being paid at all.'

'We pay your orphanage – same thing.'

'It's not *my* orphanage. I hate it.'

'Just leave then.'

'"Just do this, just do that" ... that might work for you nobles, but it doesn't work for us orphans.'

'I'm not noble.'

I started laughing. I played a clumsy, discordant arpeggio, then said: 'There you go, you played that bit. You're right – definitely not noble.'

She stood up, looking very calm. Great armfuls of sunlight came pouring in from the west. She radiated light, her white trousers like a snowy day, her arms slightly apart from her body. She breathed delicately. I didn't even know it was possible to breathe delicately. An uneducated young shepherd boy, I would have fallen to my knees before this haughty virgin. I heard Monsieur Fournier's voice again, saw his expression whenever he tapped me on the back to ask me with a knowing wink: 'So, have you seen the Virgin?' And out of the blue I thought about the encyclopaedia, that damned encyclopaedia which had set all of this in motion; I superimposed the drawing on her white trousers; I imagined *her* vulva, in living colour, in that dazzling Florentine pink of Pontormo's angels. Rose observed me. I am sure, even now, that she *knew*. Women always know. They watch us with a shake of the head as we fall – fall in love, fall from grace, fall into disrepute, freefall, fall to our death, fall to our knees ... we are always falling, those of us who have sworn to rise above it, to take the high ground.

She woke the governess.

'The class is over. You can show him out now.'

It is always in this position that I see Rose now when I think about her. Head tilted slightly, a smile masking her terror, a carnival smile that consoled and accused at the same time. And I wouldn't be surprised if it was after seeing her in the same position – her or another woman – that a small Neapolitan man with tuberculosis by the name of Pergolesi composed, almost three hundred years ago, his *Stabat mater*, before putting down his quill and falling asleep forever.

At the Baltiysky railway station in St Petersburg, around 2010, there was an incredible public piano, an old Bösendorfer. They did things properly there. I had been playing for about half an hour while waiting for my train and I had just begun the Sonata no. 9 when I heard laughter behind me. Two policemen in ushankas, their sides splitting. They weren't mocking me, they were laughing at their dogs – two German shepherds who had sat down side by side, leashes strained, heads slightly tilted, to listen to me. You will tell me that Germans have music in their blood. The dogs reacted like connoisseurs, shivering at the chromaticism in the first movement, a sign – in this supposedly minor sonata – of the greatness to come. They stayed there, completely motionless, until the end, and the policemen eventually stopped laughing and they listened too. When I had finished, one of the policemen gestured at the German shepherds and said something in Russian. Then, seeing that I did not understand, he repeated in strongly accented English: 'The dogs, them very happy.'

Shostakovich, who adored his terrier Tomka, said the reason dogs had such short lives was that they took everything too much to heart.

Pergolesi, twenty-six. Mozart, thirty-five. Schubert, thirty-one. Purcell, thirty-six. Lili Boulanger, twenty-four. And even Brian Jones, who founded the Rolling Stones, died at twenty-seven. Most of the greats do not live long. No offence to the world's coroners, but in my opinion it is always the heart that's to blame.

*

'Go on, tell us!' the others demanded the next evening. 'What was it like at that rich girl's house?'

Momo was sitting in a corner of the terrace with Asinus. He was smiling. In the space of a week, his status at the orphanage had been transformed. Weasel had sat next to him in the courtyard one morning and had *spoken* to him, and the jackals who usually tormented the little *pied-noir* at break time had backed away, muttering furiously. The little *pied-noir*, as everyone called him despite the fact he was six feet tall and had a moustache, was now under the protection of a king.

I had always thought that Momo smiled constantly. That night, I learned to stop mixing up a simple stretching of the lips – the only movement that his face could make – with happiness. When he was truly happy, you could see it in his hands, which played with the fur of his donkey instead of hanging limply by his sides. You could read it in his shortened gaze, his hypnotised eyes which forgot Oran, ceased scanning the empty horizon from the Cap de l'Aiguille and instead focused on the here and now. In these rare moments, Momo actually seemed to be with us, as if his orbit had suddenly brushed past ours. Our ellipses briefly touched before diverging once again.

'Tell us! Tell us!' the others chanted.

'Tell you what?'

'About the piano lesson. The girl.'

'Did you see her naked?' Souzix asked hopefully.

'What?! What's wrong with you?'

'You can't just see a girl naked like that,' Weasel explained magnanimously. 'It's very difficult.'

Souzix listened gravely – Weasel was the only one he really respected.

'So how do you do it?'

'It takes work. Like hunting a rare animal. You mustn't scare her away, but you mustn't hesitate either.'

'It takes work for *you*,' Sinatra sneered. 'All my dad has to do is click his fingers and the girl strips off.'

'That's true,' agreed Edison. 'It worked on your mother anyway.'

'Don't talk about my mother like that, you little snot!'

They grabbed each other by the collar and we had to separate them. Weasel turned to me.

'So are you going to tell us or not?'

'There's nothing to tell. That girl doesn't have a clue about music.'

'Just teach her then. Isn't that what you're there for?'

'It's not that simple.'

Weasel took a bar of chocolate from his pocket. He'd traded for it during the week – a delicious puffed-rice snack for which he'd had to play hardball, consolidating a whole batch of chores and selling them in bulk. He took a bite and passed it to me.

'Music's not simple?'

'No. The secret is rhythm. All the greats have it. Even the Stones.'

'Who?'

'You're kidding, right? You don't know the Stones?'

'We know Sinatra,' said Sinatra.

'He has rhythm too. Like the Stones.'

Sinatra looked surprised. I think this was the closest he had ever come to liking me. Edison had a nervous tic because he was desperate to understand.

'But what *is* this rhythm?'

'I don't know, you have to hear it.'

'Is it real?'

'Of course it's real. There's nothing more real.'

'Is it scientific?' Edison demanded. 'Does it send rockets to the stars?'

I knew the answer to this question, at least, even if it was the only one I did know.

'Of course it sends rockets to the stars.'

Rothenberg insisted, because of his leg. My mother insisted because it was a good thing to do. My father insisted because my mother insisted.

One day in February, a few months before the accident, I accompanied my old piano teacher, who had walked with a limp ever since his hip operation, to the eleventh arrondissement. This was a real pain in the arse, and I made them all aware of the fact – all except Rothenberg, because I was afraid of him – by rolling my eyes and sighing a lot. My parents travelled everywhere by car, but Rothenberg insisted that I take public transport.

In the métro carriage, he fell silent. I felt obliged to make conversation.

'Did you see that they're sending men to the moon?'

He started, and looked at me distractedly, but said nothing.

At number 2, Rue du Dahomey, an art deco facade conceals an enormous studio. *Concealed*, I should say. It has since been demolished, because it was beautiful. We rang the doorbell and a man opened the door. Severe-looking suit, haughty eyebrows. He looked down at Rothenberg, who was a head shorter than me and whose suit – which he must have bought, second-hand, in 1945 – was way too big for him. I felt terribly ashamed. The man shivered. I felt sure he was about to call the police.

He didn't call the police. He bowed so deeply he almost touched the ground.

'Monsieur Rothenberg, I didn't know you were coming today.'

He took a step to the side and clapped his hands. Two other men, who looked oddly similar, only younger, bowed us into the studio. Beneath an arachnoid metal vault, twenty or so pianos were waiting impatiently in their black livery. The wooden floorboards gleamed, two shining porcelain cups appeared on a gleaming silver platter – Rothenberg waved it away. The smell of floor polish, lacquer and varnish was making my head spin.

'Didn't Rudolf tell you I was coming?' the old leopard demanded curtly.

'Of course, Monsieur Rothenberg, but Monsieur Serkin omitted to specify which day you would be coming. Don't worry, though, it's all ready. The tuner came yesterday. We just need a few minutes to prepare it ... I think you'll be pleased.'

The man backed away. I watched Rothenberg, intrigued that this man I had known for a long time appeared to be some sort of uncrowned king.

'Why are you looking at me like that?'

'They're treating you like ... Are you a celebrity or something?'

'What did you think, that I was just an old Jew from Noisy-le-Grand? What makes you think I wasn't a famous pianist before the war? That I didn't fill concert halls all over the world and make grown men cry? What makes you think I didn't decide to stop playing because I'd had enough of it all?'

'Of course, but ...'

'I'm kidding. I really am just an old Jew from Noisy-le-Grand. But I do have a few very famous friends who trust me to choose their pianos for them.'

'But ...'

'But what?'

'If your friends are very famous and they trust you, what does that make you?'

He nodded.

'Good question.'

And that was all. He waited, hands behind his back, looking down at the parquet floor – a herringbone plain populated by black monsters. The man in the suit reappeared.

'This way, please, Monsieur Rothenberg, Monsieur.'

I almost turned around to look behind me when he addressed me as 'Monsieur'. On a stage in the middle of the room, surveying its entourage of pianos, was a Steinway Imperial. One assistant brought a stool, another a cushion. Rothenberg rejected both. He stood in front of the instrument which waited there, mouth open, jaws tensed, ready to punish the slightest error. He caressed the keyboard.

'Twelve thousand individual pieces. The wood comes from the forest where Antonio Stradivari cut *his* wood. The frame is resistant to twenty tons of tension. But it's not as valuable as all your rockets, I suppose?'

'That depends,' I replied. 'If you want to go to the moon, no.'

Rothenberg made a vague hand gesture.

'A metronome.'

They brought him a metronome. He set it to 60, looked at me and played *G sharp – C sharp – E*, three times in a row. The opening right-hand notes for Sonata no. 14.

'What is the interval between these notes, Joe?'

'Two and a half tones, and one and a half tones.'

'Very good.'

He played the same notes again, three times, at the same tempo, with no rubato, no pedal, without apparently changing anything. But they sounded very different and made me want to cry. The man in the suit had closed his eyes.

'What is the interval between these notes, Joe?'

'Two and a half tones, and one and a half tones.'

'You think it sounds the same?'

'No.'

'So what is the interval?'

'I don't understand, Monsieur Rothenberg. Between G sharp and C sharp, there's—'

'There's *metsiout*. The true reality of kabbalists, the light that connects all things. There's rhythm. You don't need a rocket to go to the moon. It's right there, at your fingertips. Ludwig was travelling through space a hundred and fifty years ago, and Bach, and Pergolesi, and Schumann, who left early for the voyage. And I shouldn't say this, but perhaps that anti-Semitic bastard Wagner went there too. All those men voyaged in a weightless state. They knew the secret names of the stars. So don't make me laugh with your rockets.'

He turned to the man in the suit.

'It's a good piano – you won't have any problems selling it. But not to Rudolf. It's not tuned.'

The man in the suit gave a pained smile.

'I don't understand. The tuner came yesterday. We could—'

Rothenberg gave an irritated sigh. His hand was trembling.

'It's tuned with itself, no doubt about that. But it's easy to be in tune with oneself, isn't it? Much harder to be in tune with that.'

He opened his arms wide, as the man watched, stupefied. Then he slapped the back of my head.

'Aren't you coming, you idiot?'

'Come on, hurry up!'

Weasel was shaking me. The others were already on their feet. The dormitory was in darkness.

'Huh? What's happening?'

The entire orphanage was creaking under the pressure of the most violent wind I had ever felt, which was tearing at it, atom by atom, with the cruel patience of someone who knows he has already won.

'We're going up,' Edison told me.

'But it's not Sunday ...'

Ignoring my objection, they walked off between the swaying walls. I followed them, still in a fog of sleep.

'What if Toad sees us?'

Toad would not see us. It was the wind bath that night, another Lookout ritual, but one so rare that I consider myself lucky to have attended it. Once every three years, a convergence of unique conditions was created between France, Spain and distant oceans, raising a synoptic wave, a terrifying rotor that would scour our valley while barely a kilometre away all was completely calm. Generations of orphans swore that, on those nights, the old priory was lifted a few centimetres from the ground before falling heavily back onto its foundations. Toad and Étienne were safely hidden away at home. It was dangerous to go out – better to wait for the next day.

The trapdoor slammed open as soon as Weasel touched it, almost torn from its hinges by a sudden gust. I was scared, really scared. Weasel climbed onto the terrace and the others followed him. Souzix held on tight to them. Momo was in the infirmary that night. He had accidentally bumped into Father Sénac in a corridor, and the priest had punished him by forcing him to eat his soup with a fork. An epileptic fit had sent Momo diving head first into his bowl. Everyone had laughed, the members of The Lookout the loudest of all, until the moment when we realised he was drowning in a puddle of turnips and potatoes.

'What the hell are we doing here?'

No sound came out of my mouth. The others burst out laughing – and no sound came out of their mouths either. Weasel crawled over to me, put his lips to my ear and yelled at the top of his voice. All I heard was a whisper.

'It's the wind bath! You can say whatever you want tonight – no one will ever know! Do what I do!'

He wedged both his feet against the angle of the terrace and the wall, opened his arms and lifted his torso up slightly. The wind raised him like a sail, then abruptly stood him upright. He struggled for a moment before returning to his original position, floating in the air at forty-five degrees. The others imitated him. Even Souzix, who – the last time they had done this, a few years earlier – had almost taken off. They had just managed to grab hold of his socks before he flew away. Souzix said he had no memory of any of this, that the others had just made it up. In fact, though, the danger was real. The wind was strong enough to carry a man away. Or to decapitate him, if a slate came loose from the roof.

Sinatra, Weasel, Edison and Souzix were now leaning into the wind, feet wedged against the low wall, arms outstretched like wings. They screamed and I didn't hear a thing. Maybe they were insulting the gods, or praying. Maybe they were pouring a flood of pure, devastating gold into the face of a sky like no sky you have ever seen before, a flood that would transform into a comet and fly off to tickle distant galaxies. It hardly mattered what we said, or didn't say. The essential thing was to roar with all your force, to empty your lungs of air and then suck in enough to last you the next three years.

It took me a while to find the right position. I fell several times, the wretched, faltering sail of a ship in a headwind. I almost gave up, but I was jealous of their dazzling, almost obscene happiness. So I kept trying, again and again, until at last I felt a huge hand take hold of me and effortlessly lift me up. I wedged myself in a hollow of that howling monster and let it rush through my open fingers. And I screamed, with every ounce of strength I had, screamed at the top of my voice, and did not hear myself make a sound. It was an incredible feeling. I yelled ' ' and ' '. I threw all my burdens to the wind.

At last I was empty, happy. Happy and intoxicated with a son's pride. I had succeeded where my parents had failed.

I was flying.

My life could have gone on like that, a life at the bottom of a valley. Today, I would be a plumber or an electrician, the only two jobs on offer to us when a local artisan needed an apprentice, couldn't find one, and, with a heavy heart, resolved to go and look for one 'up there', at Les Confins. Life could have gone on, from Saturday to Saturday, from piano lesson to piano lesson. Rose would have continued dressing in Dior, her bloodless beauty making me feel the full force of my ugliness and poverty, weighed down by second-hand shoes, almost always in shorts. At least Rose and I had reached a sort of agreement, a pact forged in the dark silence of the corridors, sealed under the cracked eyes of the cherubs on the ceiling. We hated each other. That was what we had in common, it was our mutual passion. We expected that hate from the other – her for my situation, me for her leaden fingers – and we gave it with the voracity of two lovers, in a single glance, with no need for words, as soon as I entered that reception room. I only ever opened my mouth to correct her fingering, a legato, and she to say 'thank you' in a voice that meant something else entirely. The governess always fell asleep after thirty minutes. At the sound of her first snore, Rose would vanish behind a book, ignoring me, and I would play without conviction, pretending to be two people at that piano which was so badly tuned it wasn't even in tune with itself.

Life would have gone on like that and I would have had no story to tell, I would have carried around my silence, had not Sénac – one September night when frost was burning the tiles, a night when the cold seeped out of the stones – summoned me to his office after dinner. Toad was standing to attention in a corner, his stiff leg angled slightly to one side, separated from the other in a ballet dancer's *battement*, a position of monstrous beauty. Souzix was serving the priest his evening tea. Sénac was in his favourite posture, hands joined under his chin. One finger detached itself and pointed to a seat.

'You like it here, Joseph, don't you?'

'Yes, Monsieur l'abbé.'

'Good, good. I'm pleased.'

Souzix poured the tea without spilling a drop, with the solemnity of the servant he was every Sunday.

'I was wondering something. Do you know who Jerome of Stridon was?'

'No, Monsieur l'abbé.'

'You probably know him better by the name of St Jerome. Now, do you know why St Jerome is famous?'

We all knew that. The only fresco in the church represented the scene on the wall of the apse. We stared at it every Sunday, dazed with boredom, we stared at it every holiday, we even stared at it on ordinary days, every time the priest felt like a Mass.

'He pulled a thorn from a lion's paw.'

Sénac started laughing. I had never seen him in such a good mood.

'Of course, of course. That's the legend. Jerome of Stridon is known above all, however, as the author of the first Latin translation of the Old Testament from the original Hebrew. Until then, all Latin translations had been made from other Greek translations, never from the original text. They were translations of translations, if you will. Jerome of Stridon's Bible was the first book printed by Gutenberg almost a thousand years later. Interesting, don't you think?'

'Very interesting, Monsieur l'abbé.'

'No doubt you are wondering why I have brought you here this evening just to tell you some old stories, when you would much rather go to bed. Are you wondering that, Joseph?'

'Yes, Monsieur l'abbé.'

'Well, you see, the Monseigneur has paid me the honour of asking me to write a short speech on the subject, oh, nothing too long, an hour at most, for the occasion of ... Well, never mind the occasion. But this translation of St Jerome's, commonly known as the Vulgate – I would like to know the date it was written. I don't want to make a mistake. And since you are my private secretary, a position in which I have given you my complete trust, a father's trust, I have summoned you here to help me. By chance, I have here the only volume of an encyclopaedia left behind by Father Puig when he retired, volume T–Z. I would like you to look up the word *Vulgate*.'

He *knew*. Souzix sprinkled sugar over the surface of the tea, looking very serious, as if this harmless gesture would one day take on an immense importance – *you will do this in memory of me*. I picked up the encyclopaedia and leafed through it, frowning, pretending not to know that *Vulgate* had been printed on the recto of *vulva*.

'I don't understand. I can't find it ...'

'No, you can't find it. The page was torn out. And do you know who tore out that page, for a reason as yet unknown to me?'

'No, Monsieur l'abbé.'

A vein was throbbing on Sénac's forehead, a red worm of anger that burrowed under his skin and slowly descended towards his cheek, perhaps to devour the fake smile that was still deforming it. The room began to spin before my eyes.

'Let me help you, Joseph. The only person who has access to this office—'

'It was me, Monsieur l'abbé,' Souzix announced as he handed him the cup of tea.

'I beg your pardon?'

Speechless, I stared at Souzix. Just as I had been about to leave the trench where I had taken refuge, trembling with fear, I now watched helplessly as he rode into battle on my behalf, offering his breast to the enemy. His eyes met mine and I saw in them that strange expression he sometimes wore, like a heroic old sergeant in a Hollywood film, who seemed to be saying to me: 'Don't worry, kid, it's all under control.'

'You? What on earth do you mean?' Sénac asked after a few seconds of stupefaction.

'When I came to bring you your tea the other night, you weren't here yet, and I wanted to look at some drawings ...'

'But you know that nobody is allowed to touch my belongings.'

'Yes, Monsieur l'abbé.'

'Not only did you touch my belongings, you *tore out a page*. You tore a page from my encyclopaedia.'

'Yes, Monsieur l'abbé. Because of the beaver.'

'The beaver?'

'Well, yeah. The bearded clam. The beef curtains. You know, a woman's pussy ... oh, what's it called again? Oh yeah, the vulgate.'

I wanted to laugh, to laugh until I cried – an expression that was so perfect at Les Confins, where the one activity was invariably followed by the other. There was no point confessing now. We would both be punished.

'What you did is very serious,' the priest whispered. 'Where is that page now?'

'I threw it in the bin, Monsieur l'abbé.'

'Monsieur Marthod, search the dormitory.'

Toad walked over and grabbed Souzix by his collar. Souzix collapsed like a pile of empty clothes.

'And since you seem to enjoy tearing things so much ...'

The priest opened a metal drawer and took out a blue cardboard folder.

'Your request to go on holiday in Vercors, which I had approved. As long as I am the director of this establishment, you will be wasting your time if you ever make the same request again.'

He tore up the folder. In two, in four, then sent the pieces flying. Souzix, hanging from Toad's fist, watched dolefully as his dreams of pizzas and tractor tyres scattered in sad little blue snowflakes. At a signal from the priest, Toad dragged the boy out into the corridor.

'I owe you an apology, Joseph. I thought you were the culprit.'

I had followed Toad to the doorway.

'What will he do to Souzix?'

'Monsieur Marthod will not *do* anything to him. He will simply chastise him, with the moderation of a father. As a general rule, I am opposed to corporal punishment. But sometimes one must go against one's natural inclinations for the common good. Anger can be virtuous, as Christ taught us when he overturned the tables of the money changers.'

'But, Monsieur l'abbé, he's only nine. He's a little—'

'Don't be naive, Joseph. A nine-year-old capable of such an act – tearing a page out of a book, a page of knowledge, to numb himself with lust over the representation of the female organ – cannot be described as a little boy. There is something enormous inside him. An evil that must be prevented from growing.'

The priest was right. This was all about preventing growth. And I was silent, because that prevention was of such violence that it hollowed your chest, scooped out your heart and stole your breath, forever and ever.

When it was time to go to bed, Souzix had still not returned.

In the middle of the night, there was a noise in the corridor. I was stuck in my aeroplane dream and by the time I ran over there, the other members of The Lookout were already present.

Sinatra was being the policeman, clearing away bystanders, and soon there were just the four of us around Souzix, who was sitting against the wall, his thin legs poking out of his canvas Bermudas. Blood was flowing from his right ear. Edison shook him gently; he opened his eyes and murmured: 'I fell on the stairs.'

'You didn't fall on the stairs. It's that bastard Toad. Where does it hurt?'

'I fell on the stairs.'

He bent forward and vomited, then slid down onto the floor.

'Fuck, he's really messed up. I'm going to fetch the priest.'

Weasel ran off. Souzix opened his eyes.

'Is it Sunday? The Lookout?'

'No, it's not Sunday. But we're here. It'll be okay. Where did that son of a bitch hit you?'

'I've got a bit of a stomach ache.'

His lips were blue, his forehead hot. I gently pushed back his hair.

'Why did you say it was you? The torn page, I mean?'

'Say it again? I can't hear very well ...'

'Why did you tell him you tore the encyclopaedia?'

'Did Toad find the drawing?'

'Of course not. It's safe. But why did you take the blame?'

'Because ... the day that Rose came here ... she said she'd seen *Mary Poppins* ... remember? But then, suddenly I wasn't sure I wanted to know.'

He closed his eyes. Sinatra slapped his face.

'Don't fall asleep.'

'Jesus, take it easy!' Edison shouted. 'You're worse than bloody Toad!'

'I've seen all those war films. When they close their eyes like that, it means they're about to snuff it.'

'He'll snuff it if you keep hitting him!'

Souzix had opened his eyes again. His hand reached for mine.

'I changed my mind, Joe. I really want to know. I decided to take your place, so it wouldn't stop you seeing Rose, and so you could ask her ... It's just a shame about Vercors ...'

The priest came running towards us, lights blooming in the darkness at the end of the corridor.

'You'll ask her, won't you? Ask Rose ... to tell you about the end of *Mary Poppins*. Promise me.'

'I promise.'

'You think I'm going to snuff it, lads?'

'No, of course you're not going to snuff it.'

At half past four, Souzix was admitted to the hospital in Lourdes, where the priest had taken him by car. A junior doctor diagnosed peritonitis and he was rushed into surgery. Souzix didn't snuff it, not that time. He opened his nine-year-old eyes the next morning and told the nurse that she looked like an angel, and that he was happy to be dead. After questioning the patient, the doctor attributed the peritonitis to a fall on the stairs which caused the appendix to burst, after coming out of the monitor's office where Monsieur Marthod had firmly but gently reprimanded him. Nobody could really explain the perforation of his eardrum. The doctor said it was the result of a 'phenomenon of extreme depression', which could occur from a violent collision or, as I learned later, a 'tiger's palm', a slap administered to the ear by certain experts, often military, to encourage people unwilling to talk. Souzix lost eighty per cent of the auditory faculties in his right ear.

That afternoon, from the courtyard, I saw Toad standing, head lowered, in the priest's office. Sénac was waving his arms around; he looked like he was shouting. Étienne passed behind me and looked up at the window.

'What are you looking at, lad?'

'The priest and Toad having an argument.'

The gardener laughed. 'Crows don't peck out other crows'

eyes, as my grandmother would say.'

At dinner, Sénac praised our presence of mind after our classmate's accidental fall down a staircase in Les Confins. We were allowed a glass of wine and a double helping of dessert. The priest gazed with satisfaction at our manifestations of joy. Toad was sitting in his usual place.

Five days later, Souzix reappeared, limping and slightly deaf, and was confined to his bed for several days. He was briefly treated as a hero, then life went back to normal.

On Sunday night, The Lookout had a meeting. And that was where it all began.

Souzix insisted on coming up to the roof with us. He was in so much pain that it took him ten minutes to climb the stairs, but he had already missed the trip to the mountain pasture and he regretted that. October was coming and soon the sun would leave the valley for several long months. Or, rather, it would make only brief appearances, out of courtesy, because there was so much world to illuminate and so few hours in which to do it. Souzix didn't care about the sun. But its absence meant that Camille would no longer wear those baggy vest tops she was so fond of, the neckline – stretched loose over and over again by her son's fingers – revealing mountains and valleys to make your head spin. Our youngest member had been faintly feverish ever since the business with the encyclopaedia. He still hadn't decided whether the vulva was his friend or enemy, but he accorded it the respect due to both.

I stood up to make a speech.

'This can't go on. They don't have the right to treat us like this.'

'But they do have the right,' Souzix corrected me with a lawyer's seriousness. 'They don't have the right to feel us up – I remember a teacher telling us that once. If they feel you up, you have to say no and fill out a form. But as far as slaps are concerned, they do have the right, as long as it's for our own good.'

'We're used to it,' said Weasel. 'Anyway, it's generally not too bad. That's the first time he's really hurt someone.'

'He wanted to make me admit that Joe had torn the page,' the boy explained. 'I told him he could hit me all he liked, I would never say anything to a sucker like him. That annoyed him.'

'What annoys me,' said Sinatra, 'is that until *he* arrived' – here, he pointed at me – 'everything was fine.'

Edison shook his head.

'Toad always liked hitting people.'

'But it's worse now! Like it was back in Danny's time!'

Weasel took off his beret and the four of them murmured: 'May he rest in peace.'

They were annoying me.

'What's the point of your stupid Lookout? You act all clever, but as soon as you actually have to *do* something, you back off.'

Weasel placed his hands on my shoulders.

'What exactly do you want to do? Come on, Joe the newbie, tell us what you have in mind.'

'I want to get the hell out of here. I want all of us to get the hell out of here.'

'Because you think it'd be better somewhere else?'

'I don't know. Surely it couldn't be any worse.'

He shook his head. He looked sad.

'You remind me of Danny.'

'God, I'm sick of hearing about bloody Danny. Who even was he?'

'A dreamer. Like you.'

'But taller,' said Souzix. 'And better-looking.'

'Okay, okay, I get it – he was tall and good-looking. So what happened?'

'He was full of ideas too,' Weasel explained. 'The Lookout, for example – that was him. But ideas are dangerous. The reason I know that – the same reason I know it's no better anywhere else – is that I haven't always been at Les Confins. I did six months in Brittany before I came here. One of the kids there told me: "Be a shadow," and he was right. The best way to survive, here or elsewhere, is to disappear. Not to be noticed. One day you'll get out, naturally. Until then, just don't exist and nobody will see you. You're doing the exact opposite. Just like Danny.'

'Oh, stop being so bloody mysterious! Just tell me what happened to him.'

Once again, they remembered the silence. The silence when it happened. Danny, the leader of The Lookout. Danny, protector of the weak. Nobody dared attack one of the little kids when he was around. Everyone said he was capable of killing a man, you could see it in his eyes. They said even Toad was wary of him. When Weasel reminded him to be a shadow, Danny laughed. He threw back his head and laughed, then said he would never be a shadow. He said none of them were shadows, they were starfish, from that sea they had never seen. If something cut them, mutilated them, they had to grow back what was missing.

It happened on a Sunday, in the spring of the first year, the day of their trip to the mountain pasture. The day before, Danny had been ambushed by three of the bigger boys in the toilets – three against one, that was what it took to have any hope of beating him. Afterwards, he was limping. He asked to stay behind at the infirmary. The good weather was finally returning after a long winter; they set off without him, without a second thought. Sénac, the nuns, Étienne, all of them. A wild-boar hunt forced them to turn back and return to the orphanage.

Hearing noises, they thought at first it must be a burglary. Fleeing footsteps, a slammed door. Toad grabbed a shovel and moved forward with a gracefulness they had never seen in him before. They followed him – a priest, forty kids, a few nuns and a gardener, all eager to see what would happen next. A finger to his lips, Toad pointed at the door of a box room.

He kicked it open, the shovel raised. And that was when the silence fell. Inside the cupboard was a woman. Tall, in a slightly old-fashioned flower-patterned dress, her medium-length hair hidden under a silk headscarf. The worst thing was that, when they talked about it later, they all remembered thinking: *God, she's beautiful!*

They all stared at her, petrified, devoured by her coal-black eyes, and finally they recognised Danny. Sénac ordered everyone to step back. Danny came out, trembling, head held high. The silence, the silence. They could still remember it now. Danny turned towards the dormitory. At first, no one moved. Then there were the first grunts and howls of laughter. The jeers. His enemies rushed at him and began tearing off his dress. Danny kept walking, making no attempt to defend himself against the yelling human tide that swept over him. Gaumier, the boy who spat on Momo's shoes when we first arrived, struck the first blow. Toad wanted to stop them, but Sénac held him back. Millions of furious fists and feet laid into Danny. Some hit him without knowing why, just because the others were doing it. The dinner bell had been rung, a few final weaker punches were thrown, and then they abandoned him there, breathing softly on the cold tiles in his tattered flowers.

There was an investigation. Danny had found the dress and the scarf in a wardrobe in the infirmary, left there by a novice. A piece of charcoal had been used for his make-up. Under his mattress, Toad discovered a photograph torn from a magazine during an outing to the village, the crumpled portrait of a young male singer who looked like a young female singer. His name, *David Bo*—, was ripped down the middle. No one ever really knew why Danny had dressed in women's clothes and gone walking through the corridors. Had he done it just for fun? As an act of rebellion? Because, like all good heroes, he had hidden his true identity for a long time? Or a mix of all of these? They didn't want to know, not really. All the same, there was something strange about this story: that was the opinion of a few minds whose wisdom and devotion left no room for doubt. Who would want to be a woman if no one was forcing them to do it?

When the students returned after dinner, there was no longer a pool of black, scabby blood on the floor of the corridor. Danny had disappeared.

'Disappeared!' Souzix repeated, waving his hand like a magician.

'Where did he go?'

'Come and see.'

My friends all headed towards a corner of the terrace. Étienne's cabin quivered in the blackness below, its yellow windowpanes struggling to push back the darkness. Weasel pointed at a gutter zigzagging down the back of the building.

'While we were eating dinner, Danny ran away. Even though he was in pain. He went down that way. You see? The fence passes so close to the wall that you can jump over it from that ridge. It was madness. That gutter is a hundred years old. So are the screws holding it in place.'

'And he fell to his death.'

'No. The gutter held firm, miraculously. But instead of going along the road, where he knew they would find him, he decided to climb the wall of the cirque. To escape from the bottom of the valley.'

'Without equipment? In his state?'

'Without equipment. In his state. And he died.'

'Although, it has to be said—' Edison began.

'What has to be said?' Weasel interrupted. 'Is he dead or not? That's all that matters. So, end of story. We can't leave, Joe. If we ran away, they would catch us. We can still meet here every Sunday. But escaping? Forget it.'

'Let's vote. Who wants to get the hell out of here?'

I raised my hand. I was the only one who did. I tried to catch Momo's eye – he was sitting against the low wall, gazing at the stars. He was a member of The Lookout too. A numb member, perhaps, like an arm that you have fallen asleep upon, but he was still a member, attached to the body. He had a vote, like anyone else. He smiled, but he did not raise his hand.

'Motion denied,' said Weasel.

Suddenly Edison jumped to his feet.

'A letter.'

'Huh?'

'Joe's right – this can't continue. And you're right too, Weasel – we can't leave. But we could write a letter. Explaining what happens here. Asking for help.'

The idea floated between us for a moment, a little bland but tenacious, with that strangely adult flavour of compromise. Just then, the supersonic *boom* startled me. It hadn't stopped, I had just forgotten about it, like the others. I had become one of them. I was a 'Confins boy'.

'But who could we write a letter to? We don't know anyone on the outside.'

'We know Marie-Ange,' said Edison triumphantly. 'From the radio.'

Sinatra sniggered.

'She's never even heard of you. Why would she help us? We could write to my father, of course, but with that stupid agent of his ...'

'Marie-Ange,' repeated Weasel. 'That's not such a bad idea. We can tell her that we love her show, that we listen to her every Sunday ... Women love compliments.'

'But we don't know her address.'

'Marie-Ange Roig, Sud Radio, Andorra – that's not complicated. The problem ...'

The problem was that nothing could leave Les Confins without first being censored. Stealing an envelope from the priest's office would be easy. I could do that myself. But all correspondence went to Sénac or to one of the nuns, who checked its 'moral rectitude' before dispensing the longed-for viaticum: a stamp. There was a legend that a kid who, a few years earlier, had complained in a letter about the quality of the food at Les Confins had been punished by being forced to eat whatever was sent back to the kitchen, and nothing else, for a whole month. And since nothing was ever sent back – the starving orphans ate every crumb – he had ended up losing ten of his forty kilograms. A legend.

All four of them turned to me.

'You could ask the rich girl.'

'Rose? Ask her what?'

'Next Saturday, take the letter with you. Hide it under your jumper. Ask her to put a stamp on it and post it for us.'

'You're joking! She'd never do me a favour. She thinks orphans are scum. That's why she sprays Diorling all over herself whenever I—'

'She sprays what?'

'Diorling. That's her perfume. She uses it like a disinfectant to keep the smell of me away from her precious nostrils.'

'*You know the name of her perfume?*'

There was only one possible response to this question.

'All right, I'll give her your stupid letter.'

They grinned mockingly at me. I was saved by a shooting star.

'Battle stations!' Edison shouted. 'The Russkies are attacking.'

Souzix laughed. His pain was gone. At that instant, and that instant only, nothing distinguished us from the wind or from animals; nothing separated us any longer from what ran wild and carefree along the blue line of the horizon.

The long wait among the flowers in the corridor. The long wait made worse by the letter that made me itch, that weighed a ton against my skin. The letter I didn't dare take out.

Dear Marie-Ange Roig.

The long wait made worse by the humiliation of having to ask *her* for help, that girl I hated as I had never hated anyone before, not even my unbearable sister when she put my Monkees record in the oven 'to see if it was made of liquorice'.

We are The Lookout.

The manor house was silent. I imagined myself having been forgotten there, the family having left for Paris. Nobody had thought about the orphan in the corridor, the one who came on those slow Saturdays, and by the time they realised that he was missing, if not missed, it would be too late. My heart began to pound.

We are a group of students from the boarding school Les Confins. We listen to you every Sunday – you have a very beautiful voice. We are writing to you because you are the only one who can help us.

A spray of carnations faced me, in its black frame. A door slammed somewhere in the house. So I hadn't been forgotten ... I exhaled.

The chief monitor here is a violent man. Several students have been injured. We don't know who to tell. But you will know – you must know lots of important people because you're on the radio. If you receive this message, say the word 'Lookout' on your show on Sunday night because that is the only night we are able to listen to you. With our sincere gratitude, dear sister in Christ ...

I had convinced them to use the priest's usual sign-off – it clearly worked, to judge from the flood of donations. The 'boarding school' was my idea too. If you're looking for a helping hand, it's better to hide the fact that you're a leper.

A shadow detached from the rest, to my left. A man walked past me, a small grey man in a small grey suit, carrying a small grey briefcase. He nodded almost imperceptibly at me then disappeared to my right. Silence again. At last the governess appeared and, trotting along on her cork heels, led me to the reception room. Nothing had moved since the previous Saturday, or the Saturdays before that. Nothing had moved there for centuries: not Rose, sitting at the end of the piano bench, nor the asthmatic angels who were suffocating on the ceiling, their conch shells, their oboes d'amore and their lungs all heavy with the greasy soot spat out for years by the fireplace.

She opened the score, the crackle of paper breaking the silence. Bach. I sight-read the *Goldberg Variations*. Rose imitated me, like a clumsy, sluggish, half-asleep puppy following its master. Her forehead was a little shiny. The rhythm was far away – from me as much as from her. The governess, sitting up straight in her armchair, listening attentively, refused to fall asleep for once. I couldn't take out the letter with her watching. When the hour was up, a little bell rang somewhere in the bowels of the house. The old lady leapt up, smoothed down her skirt, and nodded at us before exiting the room. I immediately took off my jumper. Rose watched, open-mouthed.

'What are you doing? If you think—'

I handed her the letter. I had been rehearsing this conversation all week, playing the scene over and over in my head, Hollywood-style, leaving nothing to chance. *I know we've had our ups and downs, baby, mostly downs* … It didn't sound quite so good in French, but it would do. *But it's time to forget all that. I have a favour to ask you.*

'I want you to post this.'

'You *want*?'

'Yes. We can't do it ourselves.'

'What is it?'

'A letter.'

'I can see it's a letter. Why don't you post it yourself? Do you think I'm your secretary or something?'

'It's a letter we can't post ourselves.'

'Why not?'

'Because we live on the moon, you understand?'

'I understand that you're completely crazy.'

'Will you post it, yes or no?'

'No.'

Sounds from behind the door. I was so shocked, I didn't even think about hiding my letter. There must have been some technical hitch – the wrong subtitles or the wrong film, the details didn't really matter. The door handle turned. Rose grabbed the envelope from me and slipped it inside the score, which she closed.

'Don't think I'm doing this for free.'

The count and his wife entered, the former with his perpetually preoccupied expression of a man with more important things to think about, the latter with the stumbling, swaying gait of someone walking along a mountain ridge. Sénac followed them into the room. Behind them, further back, last and very much least, a shepherd appeared. A strange-looking shepherd, whose furnace-red habit and golden staff guided multitudes across the slopes of night. Beneath his mitre, he smiled like a tired child, as if apologising for having worn this disguise too long. He would, in fact, give it up a few months later.

'Monseigneur Théas, this is young Joseph Marty, one of our boarders,' announced Sénac. 'He volunteered to give piano lessons to Mademoiselle Rose.'

I bent down to kiss the bishop's ring – I had at least learned a few manners through working for the priest – but he kept my hand in his and put his other hand on my forehead. Then whispered, for my ears only: 'God bless you, Joseph.'

I once saw my parents vaporised, my sister go up in flames, returning to the stars the atoms she had borrowed to become herself, Inès, while I remained whole. I have had my share – more than my share – of gods who bless, of one-true-god-creator-of-heaven-and-earth, of resurrections of the flesh, of sons seated at the father's right hand, of the litanies of saints. The only father's right hand I know is the one my friends and I received, right in the kisser. I saw a thousand men broken by a life lived in black and white. And charlatans promising them, at the Sunday market, that if they believed with all their heart and didn't ask too many questions, one day they would live life in colour.

But when Théas whispered: 'God bless you,' I believed it for the one and only time in my life, because – unlike the others – he believed it too.

Rose made the same outmoded curtsey she had made to Sénac, that first day. Her parents gestured us towards the sofas.

'Monseigneur Théas has generously brought us a cake,' the count declared. 'What do we say, Rosette?'

His daughter stared at him incredulously.

'We say thank you, I suppose,' she replied in a cold voice.

Sénac froze, but the count did not seem to have noticed his daughter's insolence.

'Thank you, Monseigneur,' the priest corrected her with a tense smile.

The bishop gave a weary wave. 'No need for formalities. Shall we try the cake? I wish I could claim I made it with my own hands, but as you can see' – he showed us his gloved hands – 'I am poorly equipped.'

The count was about to ring the bell, but the priest stopped him with a movement of his hand.

'Joseph can do the honours, if that is all right with you. Our boarders are raised to serve the glory of God in all circumstances. Joseph?'

I nodded, ridiculously grateful to Sénac because he'd called us *boarders*.

The kitchen was at the end of the corridor, and even darker than the rest of the house. Perhaps, once, the sun had attempted to penetrate it by force, but it had got lost in this labyrinth where its lifeless body turned slowly white. On a scarred table, near a pile of dirty dishes, an apple tart was waiting in an enormous cardboard box stamped *Central Bakery*. In the flickering light of a single bulb, I transferred most of the portions to the largest of the dishes.

Just as I was about to leave the kitchen, I spotted the notebook. An unfinished grocery list, which ended with *aspirin*. On top of the notebook was a felt-tip pen. And the idea came to me, the idea that could derail everything. Dangerous, exciting. I was putting The Lookout in peril, but I didn't care about that. The letter was pointless, I felt sure. The solution was to hit back – as hard as they hit us. I picked up the felt-tip pen and wrote *HELP!* on the underside of the cake box lid. I went over each letter, to make them stand out. Then I closed the lid, leaving the box next to the sink, where someone would open it after our departure. Where someone would find, instead of a little sweetness, the darkness of a grave. I returned to the reception room, the dish shaking slightly in my hands, and served the tart. The men were talking, the women silent. The bishop gave me a friendly wink – a fraction of a second of his attention, a fraction of a second that caused the space to expand and filled it, making me understand why so many streets and squares would, years later, bear his name. Rose, visibly bristling, ate without looking up.

The conversation dried up, bitten in the heart by one of those silences that prowled around the old house.

To fill the immense void that followed, Sénac announced: 'Joseph refused to be adopted by a host family. He preferred to remain at Les Confins. Isn't that right, Joseph?'

I opened my mouth. Nothing came out, other than a piece of apple which fell onto my plate, earning me a contemptuous sneer from Rose. The bishop turned towards me.

'*Isn't that right, Joseph?*' Sénac repeated.

His smile grew even wider. It was a false, lopsided smile, forged without joy in some lightless foundry.

'Yes, Monsieur l'abbé.'

'What led you to make such a choice, my boy?' asked Monseigneur Théas.

Sénac placed a friendly hand on the back of my neck and tousled my hair.

'Don't be shy, Joseph. Tell the bishop what you told me that day. That your family is Les Confins now. Isn't that what you said?'

'Yes, Monsieur l'abbé. That is what I said. My family is Les Confins now.'

The silence, once again, snapped its bony jaws under the high ceiling.

'More tart?' suggested the countess. 'There must be some left in the kitchen. Joseph, would you bring the box in please?'

All eyes turned to me.

'You were spoken to,' murmured Sénac.

'Yes. Yes, there is some left, but ...'

'But what?'

Luckily, Théas stood up.

'Not for me, thank you. I should be on my way. My flock awaits. I would have liked to hear you play the piano,' he said, looking at me and Rose, 'but that will have to wait for another day.'

'And I fear we have abused your hospitality too long already,' added the priest, imitating his superior.

I was shaking so hard that I had to shove my hands into my pockets. The walk to the front door seemed endless to me, the corridors longer and gloomier than ever. On the doorstep, we said our farewells to the count. Just as we were about to leave, however, we heard the sound of footsteps rushing through the house.

'Wait! Don't leave yet!'

Rose's mother appeared, out of breath, brandishing the cake box, that damned box with its dangerous message written in capital letters inside. After getting her breath back, she handed the box to Sénac.

'You should take the rest, Father. Give it to the orphans.'

'Keep it!'

The words had come out of my mouth, so loud they almost constituted a yell. Sénac turned to me, his face impassive.

'I mean, um … there is some left, but not enough.'

I was drenched, sweating so hard that I was about to melt completely, to trickle down the stone steps and sink into the dry, indifferent earth of the Pyrenees. And yet, when I touched my forehead, it was dry. Sénac's eyes bored slowly into mine.

'It is very kind of you, my dear friend. Our orphans will be grateful.'

He took the box. Toad stubbed out the cigarette he was smoking and drove the car forward. Sénac got in the back seat and signalled for me to join him. He was giving off a sweetish, chemical smell. He had dyed his temples that morning.

We drove through the village. Toad went slowly, far too slowly, the windows open. Beside me, the priest drummed his fingers on the cardboard box sitting in his lap. *Don't look at the box. Look straight ahead.*

Straight ahead of me was Toad's back, higher and wider than the passenger seat. A back covered in hair, some of which, thick and twisted, burst out from under his shirt collar and merged with the flat, strangely fine hair on his head, in a fluvial confluence facilitated by his lack of a neck, a pileous delta that made me feel instantly nauseated.

No, look at Sénac instead, as if nothing's wrong. Smile, it'll look more natural. Don't look at the box.

I looked at the box.

Sénac looked down at the box, then up at me, then down at the box again. He shrugged, forgetting me, and delicately smoothed the hair on his temples, which had been ruffled by the breeze.

'It was a very nice tart, wasn't it, Joseph?'

'Yes, Monsieur l'abbé.'

'Would you like another slice?'

'No, Monsieur l'abbé.'

'Are you sure?'

'Yes, Monsieur l'abbé.'

'Hmm, *I'm* not sure ...'

The priest caressed the lid, opened it partway, examined me from beneath it, then let it fall shut again.

'You think I don't know, Joseph?'

He tapped Toad's shoulder.

'Stop here.'

Toad parked by the verge, on the edge of town, next to an old metal skip. Sénac's hot breath, stinking of bitterness and apple, enveloped my face, choking me as overpoweringly as a chief monitor on a stormy night.

'You think I don't know that you're a glutton?'

He tossed the cardboard box through the open window and it

flew straight into the skip. He signalled to Toad. The DS set off again.

'Gluttony is a deadly sin. You see, Joseph? Today, the Lord had something to tell you.'

Souzix was eagerly awaiting me when I returned to Les Confins. He wanted to know how it had gone, did I know the end? The end of *Mary Poppins*, which I had forgotten to ask Rose about. So I made something up. A story about children sent to an orphanage secretly funded by the Russians, and how Mary Poppins flew in on an umbrella and rescued them. Souzix's eyes were like saucers and he punched the air as I described each fight, especially the final combat between Mary Poppins and the priest Rasputin.

I passed over the cake fiasco in silence – I'd been compared to Danny enough already. Danny, Danny, Danny ... I'd had enough of their hero and his legendary acts of daring. Indeed, legend had it that he had been born in an orphanage, the fruit of an illicit love affair between a nun and a layperson, because in such places all love is illicit. Danny was huge, according to Souzix. He wasn't really all that huge, Sinatra argued. Souzix said that he was strong, capable of strangling a wild boar with one hand, and that his hands were as big as frying pans. The others laughed: they had never seen Danny strangle a boar, with one hand or two. But when it came to his temper, his fits of fury, they all agreed on those. No one messed with Danny. He was brave, selfish and crazy.

After many delays, they showed me a photograph of him which they kept as a relic. It had been taken during one of Danny's numerous adventures, a nocturnal escape to the village, which he undertook to win a bet. As if climbing over the wall were not enough, he had the audacity to go to the local bar. As proof, he brought back a Polaroid of himself, taken by a couple of hikers: a handsome boy with shoulder-length hair, in a red T-shirt, staring directly into the lens. It was a strange kind of proof. Because, if you looked closely, the boy in the photograph was not really there, in that bar, standing against that sad wood-panelled wall. It was the portrait of an absence. Danny's eyes, beneath his long, feminine lashes, were not looking at the camera. They were looking far beyond it, through the viewfinder, through the photographer, through space, travelling all around the world before coming back to himself. And perhaps even then, perplexed by some sixth sense, by the iridescent gentleness of his masculinity, Danny was thinking: *One day I will leave, I'll leave for good*.

Every night the following week, Souzix woke me just as I was falling asleep.

'Joe, Joe, you think it worked? You think Marie-Ange received it? The letter?'

The first night, I answered him with that tenderness peculiar to orphans:

'Oh, fuck off.'

He wet his bed, and wore the Cape of Piss the next morning. While we waited for Sunday, when we would finally be able to listen to *Crossroads of the Night*, I had to tell him each night where the letter was at that moment. In the postman's van, with its odour of oil. At the sorting centre, with its smell of sweat. It was driven over a rain-scented col – Souzix had an olfactory obsession. Thursday: the letter made its way down towards Andorra. Friday: the postman dropped it into his leather-perfumed satchel and began his rounds.

'Joe, Joe, is it there? Has Marie-Ange received it now?'

On Friday, I drew the story out. The postman stopped for a smoke. He changed a wheel. He lost his car keys. Souzix became enraged, yelling at the postman to hurry up. On the last night, Saturday, I gave Souzix the best possible present.

'That's it, the letter arrived today. Marie-Ange should have opened it by now.'

He could hardly breathe.

'Really? Are you sure? What do you think she said?'

'She didn't say anything. It's a secret between us and her. Maybe someone pointed out to her that she had a strange expression on her face and asked her what was going on. She replied: "Nothing, nothing," and she folded our letter and hid it under her dress, pressed against her naked skin. She's thinking now.'

Souzix did not sleep a wink that night. The next day, he fell asleep in the middle of Mass. Toad yanked him from the bench and, to help him repent, gave him a 'baptism in the waters of the Jordan', a technique consisting of shoving the penitent's head underwater, just a little longer than necessary, in the cold fountain outside Les Confins.

That night, at ten o'clock precisely, Weasel turned the knob of our radio on the terrace. The opening credits began. Marie-Ange smiled silently from inside the radio. We held our breath.

She did not pronounce the word 'lookout'.

We lay down on the terrace, side by side, under the flag of stars for those fallen in battle.

'She mustn't have received the letter,' Weasel decided. 'Look at those mountains over there. The col is covered with mist. It's bound to slow everything down.'

'You're right. I'm sure she'll get it this week.'

To console us, Sinatra offered to tell us about Vegas. In truth, we all knew his tales of Vegas by heart and it wouldn't console anyone but him, but we didn't argue. There was just the faintest, tiniest, purely statistical possibility that Frank really was his father, particularly since there was a strange resemblance between the two of them. But whether that resemblance was the consequence or the cause of this whole story, it was impossible to say. And since Sinatra had promised to invite us all to Vegas if his father's Jewish agent ever stopped scheming, we tended to think it was better to play along, just in case. After all, the shopkeeper from Figeac, now staring at the wall in a psychiatric hospital far from here, had perhaps been telling the truth.

So Sinatra started to speak. About Sin City, the city without clocks, a daze of neon lights, greens and yellows and pinks, its noisy streets and its eternal palm trees. We followed him past a line of women with Medusa eyes. The women hated us. They yelled: 'Why do *they* get to skip the queue?' A huge bouncer tried to stop us at the door to the casino. But a small man in an old-fashioned suit, who looked like Rothenberg, slapped the back of his head. 'Show some respect, you idiot, that's Frankie's son and his friends.' This news silenced the Gorgons. We were shown to our table in the VIP section, just in front of the stage. A man was already sitting there. He shook our hands and introduced himself in a deep voice, a voice that spoke of moons that were blue and hotels full of broken hearts. 'Hey kids, I'm Elvis.' Souzix ordered a glass of cold milk, Momo an anisette, and the rest of us asked for whisky. Frank appeared, his collar askew, and Vegas sighed. He winked at us, started singing his latest hit, 'My Way', and all was well.

The week began with its whistle blasts, its morning prayers, its silent meals, yet more whistle blasts, more silences, frost on the windows, cold in the stones, the usual chores, and Weasel's deals. A new arrival: a dishevelled five-year-old who kept looking around in perpetual astonishment. The next day, he was wearing the Cape of Piss, shivering in the courtyard, more astonished than ever. And what did my friends do when they saw him pass, yellow and numb with cold, in front of the window? They mocked him, of course, Souzix loudest of all. Like I said, they weren't saints.

Boredom, squeezing us like a vice. We excavated our chests, searching within for the space that did not exist outside us. Even the classes weighed us down, heavy with a vacuity that would have horrified my mother, the teacher. Nobody tried to educate us, only to keep us busy. They had to make sure we were capable of choosing between electricity and plumbing. That we could tell the difference between a phase wire and a neutral wire, a slip connector and a crimp connector. We were not taught to think about the bigger picture. We were always put next to the socket and the tap, never at the other end of those copper arteries that illuminated our nights or quenched our thirst, never at the gushing springs, the magnificent turbines. That is why we were poor plumbers, bad electricians.

That week, Edison rebelled. He went to find the priest and asked him to get us some mathematics textbooks more advanced than the ones we were using – he sensed a beauty there that escaped us. The priest laughed, and so did Toad. The monitor pointed out that Edison was lucky to be educated like a real French person and that he was unlikely to need maths to sweep the streets. The priest reprimanded Toad. The colour of your skin was of no importance in the eyes of God, as long as you were a good Christian. But, he added, a good Christian had no need to learn advanced mathematics, otherwise the Bible would have said so. But didn't Jesus show a fondness for multiplication? Edison retorted. Sénac made him scrub the outside toilets – the worst ones – to teach him humility. And to ensure his contrition, to make sure he did not relapse, Toad baptised him several times in the waters of the Jordan.

The next day, Wednesday morning, the monitor came into our class and pointed at Sinatra.

'You. With me.'

'Me?'

'Yeah, you. Are you deaf or what? With me, I said. Monsieur l'abbé wants to see you.'

Sinatra shot us a worried look. Weasel ignored him, Edison ignored him, Souzix ignored him. I ignored him too. Every man for himself. Momo ignored him, but I couldn't have sworn that he really understood what was happening. The class dragged on endlessly beneath the cracked plaster ceiling. Sinatra came back, pale-faced, just before the bell. Momo elbowed me in the ribs and showed me a flower he'd just drawn.

The bell rang. We exited in single file, Sinatra the last in line. At the refectory, he sat apart from us. He ate absent-mindedly, frowning slightly. We had PE after lunch, but on the way there he stopped to go to the toilet. Weasel left the group to follow him in, and I followed Weasel. Edison, full of fresh humility and a slight case of bronchitis, decided it was better not to go with us.

Sinatra was standing at the urinal when we burst into the bathroom which, despite the windows open all year round, despite all the scrubbing by kneeling sinners, always stank of urine – the piss of malnourished monks or obese canons, of shivering kids and hormonal teenagers, a yellow odour that had become embedded in every joint and held the building together like glue. He was staring at the ceiling, his mouth half open.

'What the hell happened?' Weasel shouted.

Sinatra, startled, sent a jet of piss against the wall, spraying decades of crude art: hearts pierced by arrows, promises of French Algeria, *René + Jean-Louis*, spurting penises, death to the FLN, all of it fading into oblivion. He corrected his aim, then shook and zipped up his trousers. When he turned to us, he was smiling.

'Are you ready?' he asked.

'For what?'

'For this: my father replied.'

'What?'

'Well, his agent did. He said Frank wants to do some tests to see if I'm his son. They're going to send someone. Some kind of expert.'

'You're kidding.'

'No. The priest told me.'

'When's he coming, this expert?'

'I don't know. But it'd better be soon. I don't want to rot here.'

He started laughing, nervously, laughing louder and louder, until soon he couldn't stop. When, at last, he got his breath back, he put his hands on his hips and puffed out his chest.

'You weren't expecting that, were you?'

Then he left, shaking his head and whistling 'My Way'.

'You think it's possible?' Weasel muttered. 'That Sinatra's his dad?'

'I dunno. I mean, they do look alike ...'

'I'm just going to wait for the test results.'

'Me too.'

We joined the others, still a little flabbergasted, our eyes full of the Strip's bright lights, the taste of all-you-can-eat lobster and T-bone steak in our mouths. It was inconceivable. It was illogical.

But we had seen more unbelievable things before, and we would see others in the future too.

It was raining cats and dogs. And not skinny little Siamese or chihuahuas either. These were Amur tigers and Great Danes, English mastiffs and Barbary lions pouring down on us. Toad took a malign pleasure in parking the DS as far as possible from the count's house.

'Could we get a bit closer?'

'The driveway's full of mud. You don't expect me to get my tyres dirty, do you?'

I ran three hundred metres under a curtain of hail. Inside, I stood there shivering amid the flowers, half dazed, as I waited for Rose. An hour passed.

When I was finally admitted, I saw a fire burning in the hearth. I went over to it, as much to warm up as to dry my sweater. The governess was not with us. Presumably she had realised that no one was ever going to write an opera about us – and she was right. Rose, sitting on the bench, turned in my direction. She was wearing the same poppy-red dress she had worn on the first day.

'Haven't you ever heard of an umbrella?'

'Did you post our letter?'

'*Hello, Rose. How are you, Rose?* Don't they teach you good manners in your *orphanage*?'

She had emphasised the last word, to hurt me. She burst out laughing.

'What's good about us is that we hate each other and we can say anything at all without fear of upsetting each other. You think I'm stuck-up, spoiled, too rich, too this, too that. You don't like the way I dress.'

'I do like the way you dress,' I corrected her quietly. 'Marc Bohan is a genius.'

I was only repeating what my mother used to say. I knew nothing about genius back then, other than what I'd heard others say. But I did genuinely like that dress. It corseted and liberated her at the same time. I looked at its shady folds and wished I could lose myself, exhaust myself in them. Rose was silent. She looked staggered. I couldn't have surprised her more if I'd pulled a bouquet of flowers from her ear, as I'd seen a magician do at my sister's last birthday party. Inès had screeched with joy. She had not had many birthdays.

Taking advantage of her surprise, I hit her while her guard was down.

'But the rest is true. Stuck-up, spoiled, too rich. And you wear too much perfume.'

She laughed again. This time her lips were white, even whiter than usual. She quickly counterattacked.

'And you smell of wet sheep.'

'It's this stupid jumper. It's soaked.'

'No, Joseph. You smell of wet sheep all the time, even when you're not wearing that stupid jumper, even when it's not raining. You're unpleasant, miserable and selfish. We can tell each other all this quite openly, can't we? It's so nice not to have to pretend.'

'Have you ever pretended?'

'I pretend all day long. I pretend so much that, even now, I'm pretending. Pretending to bear your presence. The truth is that I'd like to push you into the fire.'

I turned towards the hearth. I wanted to atomise myself too. Scatter my atoms in a whirl of anger on this October afternoon that looked like night.

'Did you post our letter or not?'

'Yes, I posted your letter.'

'Are you sure?'

'Do you want a receipt or what?'

Having warmed up a little, I took my place at the piano.

'All right, today we're going to study—'

'No, today, *you're* going to study. Play for both of us. Make it sound like I'm improving – my parents will be happy. Especially my father. He doesn't like spending his money for no return. I'm going to read. So try to make my progress gradual. And stop looking at me like you're some poor beaten dog.'

I owed her. So I played. Or, rather, I touched the keys, which moved a hammer, which struck a string which emitted a note, a note that was then integrated into a melody, a harmony, or both. This was not music. Rose watched me from over the top of her book.

'It's funny,' she murmured.

'What's funny?'

'You've never played like you did that first day, in the priest's office.'

I didn't find that funny, not at all. I found it disturbing that she had noticed it.

'I don't remember playing any differently then.'

'Oh you did. If you played like that again, I'd recognise it right away, even if I heard you from the other side of the world. Where did you hear about Marc Bohan?'

She closed her book. She jumped from one subject to another with the recklessness of a trapeze artist. I tried to look smug.

'Everybody knows Marc Bohan.'

'No, they don't. It was your mother, wasn't it? What did they do, your parents?'

Two months of indifference and suddenly I was being machine-gunned from all angles. The earth was quaking, my mouth was dry with fear. Light poured through the windows, streaking the air silver. I fought back a furious urge to run away.

'The shoes your father wears, his Oxfords ... My father makes them. Made. Well, he didn't make them himself, it was his company that made them. That and mattresses.'

'How did your parents die?'

Stabat mater dolorosa
Juxta crucem lacrimosa
Dum pendebat Filius.

'You don't want to talk about it?'

The mother stood, in pain, in tears, close to the cross where her son was hanging. Her deformed son, her son dented by thorns, the black gouache mixed with blood, sweat, tears, the gouache that scratched out his face and then that crooked mouth, dribbling vinegar over cheap paper. Giovanni Battista Pergolesi had turned it into the tenderest music ever heard. And me? I had laughed. Laughed at a man's misery.

'Plane crash.'

'Hmm.'

No 'sorry' or 'that's so terribly sad, poor Joseph'. Just 'hmm'. And she didn't speak to me again – not only that day, but for months afterwards – except to say hello, thank you, goodbye. I was grateful to her for that. Hate, like prayer, feeds on silence.

The next evening, Marie-Ange again did not say the word 'lookout'. She did not say it the Sunday after that either, nor the one after that. It was time to face facts: our letter had got lost, or someone else had opened it first and thought it was a prank. We preferred not to imagine that she could have read it and done nothing.

November came, damp and grey and blade-like, and we looked out through windows trickling with condensation. The big boiler in the basement had started working again: we could hear it roaring through the stone floor. The coal chore was added to the roster, to Toad's delight – because it allowed him to joke, every time he saw Edison: 'Oh, were you scooping coal today?' before walking off, leaving behind the sound of his throaty smoker's laugh. The chore consisted in transporting the black rocks from the coal chute to the monster's mouth, and at first I was amazed by the ardour with which the little kids performed this task. They pushed whole wheelbarrows of the stuff, each child holding one of the handles, sometimes aided by a third, while the older boys watched in satisfaction. Apparently those older boys had told the younger ones that if there wasn't enough coal in the furnace, *they* would be thrown into the flames. A small orphan burns for a long time, they were told, and produces a wonderfully gentle heat, much sought-after by all the world's ogres.

Sinatra was on edge. He would jump whenever a car horn honked outside the gate. But it was never the promised expert, just the industrial baker that delivered our bread, or the truck that brought our coal, or – once – a German family who had got lost and thought this must be their hotel.

'Another of the Jew's tricks,' he muttered.

'What have the Jews ever done to you?' I asked.

'They've stopped me seeing my father – that's what they've done. And now they're delaying the expert.'

Edison – who rarely opened his mouth and whose thoughts were all about circuits, electrical charges, positive, negative – opened his mouth.

'Will you ever shut up?'

'Who the fuck asked you? Go back to Africa.'

'I'm from the Jura, you fat moron!'

Edison flew at Sinatra and they fought. Once they had been separated, the two of them grudgingly shook hands, watched by our tacit leader, Weasel. Sinatra admitted that he didn't really have anything against the Jews. Edison conceded that Sinatra wasn't fat.

The Lookout continued to meet even in the worst weather. Weasel had bartered with Étienne for a piece of tarp and we lay underneath it when it rained. It was narrow, stifling, but at least it kept us dry. We listened to our radio in the glow of a bulb stolen from a corridor, which Edison lit up with a circuit of potatoes. One dark night, under a sky filled with clouds threatening snow – the first Sunday of Advent 1969 – Marie-Ange whispered, as the programme was ending: 'And whatever you do, if you're on the roads tonight, look out for patches of ice.' Six hearts leapt in unison – yes, even Momo's, because we had been so startled that we startled him too. There was a long debate over whether the verb really counted, since it broke the name of our secret society in two. But when you thought about it, 'lookout' was not a common word. Perhaps this was the only way she could find to include it without sounding odd? The more we talked about it, though, the less sure we felt. Gradually, our enthusiasm dimmed. And since nothing happened in the weeks that followed, we were forced to admit that it must have been merely a coincidence.

*

On the last Sunday of Advent, as was traditional, the entire orphanage went down to the village. The bus parked on a paved esplanade near a waterfall at the edge of town, then we walked in procession behind a large papier-mâché star. The priest led the way. After this, we were free to come and go as we liked around the village square, a freedom strictly limited by Toad who, like a perverse sheepdog, patrolled in wide circles, bringing any strays back into the fold by kicking them with his hobnailed boots. When it came to finding us even in the darkest, narrowest alleys and expelling us, Toad had no equal.

We were ghosts. I was never so aware of the fact as I was on that particular night. The villagers smiled and applauded as we passed. But they didn't *see* us. All they saw was the priest smiling, shaking their hands, and the members of his entourage: a few nuns, and Rachid and Camille, who had volunteered to come along. They didn't see the little new boy stumbling along at the front of our spectral horde. Their gazes hovered vaguely above our heads. With no past, no future, no before and no after, an orphan is a one-note melody. And there is no such thing as a one-note melody.

The only times we gained even a semblance of substance were when we entered a shop. Then they would squint and, with a superhuman effort, manage to make out a vague shape which they did not look at directly, as if unsure of exactly where it was located. The longer we stayed in the shop, the more money we spent, the more daring they grew, even taking our cash without flinching and handing us back the sweets, posters or magazines we had asked for.

And then we would disappear through the door, leaving behind a vibration in the air, a crepuscular impression, but no footprints in the snow. And if by chance we ever did leave any footprints, they were quickly swept away. The villagers closed their shutters, perhaps they thought *poor kids*, and then, almost instantly: *glad I'm not one of them.*

'We do not talk about politics at the table,' my father taught me. 'Nor do we discuss sex or religion.'

He had learned this from his mother, and it was good advice. During the Christmas dinner at the orphanage, which took place in the refectory, illuminated by dozens of candles, we did not talk about politics – and certainly not about sex. We did, however, talk about religion. A lot. The priest himself had taken his place at the lectern and he stood up between each course to read out a passage from the Gospel. We were shaking with hunger and impatience after the two-hour Mass we had just endured at the Dominican convent. Sénac commanded us to have joy in our hearts, our souls lifted up by exultation. What we actually had was bellies whining with emptiness.

The menu was no different from usual, with the exception of a sticky brioche bun, decorated with candied fruit, which the industrial bakery had delivered three days earlier. That was our dessert. The ration of wine had been doubled for the over-sixteens. We secretly gave the little kids some to drink. The bakery had also delivered a crate of conical hats and paper streamers, which had been dumped in the furnace. It was Christmas, the priest reminded us, not carnival. But the inhabitants of Les Confins appeared happy. Sénac himself had seemed cheerful, almost carefree, all day long.

'Why do you look so miserable?' Weasel whispered to me.

'Because at my last Christmas we had turkey. And a Yule log.'

'At my last Christmas, the building collapsed on us.'

We were told we could leave. It was almost midnight and the bitingly cold air was heady with the scent of resin and pine cones. Toad, who had come down with a hellish case of flu following the trip to the village, was muttering to himself while he stamped his feet in the fresh snow. He watched us, his head held back, as if incapable of fully opening his eyelids. The sound of bells reached us, twelve chimes carried our way by a snowy gust at the tip of a steeple. A muffled joy stirred in our hearts, the joy of a manger, of animals talking at midnight, while in the East three shepherds followed a star. Those who had heard the words in a previous life murmured 'Merry Christmas', and a few eyes glistened. I elbowed Momo.

'Hey … Merry Christmas, mate.'

He nodded excitedly several times and buried his lips between Asinus's ears to silently tell him about dates stuffed with marzipan, *oreillettes* dripping with grease, *roscos* fragrant with anis and orange blossom, the delicious scents of Christmases past.

Sénac clapped his hands for silence.

'A saviour is born to us – hallelujah! hallelujah!'

'Hallelujah!' shouted a few brown-nosers.

'This time of joy and reflection, of abasement before the greatest of miracles, is also a time of forgiveness. The most sinful of all sinners, the one whose name you have expunged from your memories, expressed to me this morning his desire for repentance. He begged me on his knees to be allowed to return to the bosom of the Church. What father could refuse?'

A murmur of excitement ran through the courtyard.

'Satan bowed down before the power of Christ. It is time to welcome the lost sheep back from oblivion!'

Weasel had turned white. Some of the other kids were hopping up and down, and one of the little ones started to cry hysterically.

'What's going on?'

Weasel, vacant-eyed, ignored my question.

'Follow me, Les Confins!'

Sénac's cheeks were red with cold and his face was transformed by a joyfulness I had never seen in him before. Followed by a disorderly crowd of orphans, and the staggering Toad, he headed towards the dormitory. He went past it, took a heavy key from his pocket and unlocked the metal door through which he had disappeared on the night I discovered The Lookout. The hysterical kid wept even louder when he saw the staircase vanishing into darkness and he froze, refusing to take another step. The happy mob parted around him and went on, paying no attention to him or to the puddle that was spreading across the floor between his feet.

You think you know everything and you know nothing. You think you know everything about Les Confins, about the madness of men, but what little I know about it, I learned at Christmas 1969 when we walked down that staircase to the basement. It was a different basement from the one, hewn from yellow stone, that housed the boiler. The old priory must have been built on existing foundations. A breeze-block corridor, with archways to one side sealed off by grating, led to a metal door. The corridor was clean, the floor concrete; it was lit at regular intervals by bulbs hanging from a black cable on the ceiling. I was expecting to smell damp, like some old dungeon, but what I breathed in was incense, as if the smoke from the Dominican Mass, weighed down by all the petitions, had descended underground instead of rising to the sky. Maybe that was why God had not answered.

'Where are we?' I asked Souzix.

'Oblivion.'

This time I heard it: the capital letter at the beginning of the word. *It is time to welcome the lost sheep back from Oblivion.* The boarders lined up either side of the door at the end of the corridor. Sénac waited a few seconds, then opened it with a second key.

Nothing happened.

'Don't be afraid,' the priest said. 'Come.'

A man emerged, blinking. His head had been recently shaved

– it still bore the stripes left by the avenging clippers – while his face was half invisible under a beard.

He stepped forward into the light. What I had thought a beard was only the shadows pooling in the hollows of his cheeks. And he wasn't a man. He wasn't an adolescent either, though, not with eyes like that. And since he had never been a child, since none of the inhabitants of Les Confins ever had been, I thought for a moment that I was admiring some kind of alien creature. I recognised him only because of his red T-shirt. The same T-shirt he'd been wearing in the one and only photograph I'd seen of him, except that the red could only be guessed at in the magmatic stripes under the layer of grime that blackened the fabric.

'Go ahead. Tell your comrades what you told me this morning.'

'I'm sorry,' breathed the alien.

'Louder,' the priest barked.

'I'M SORRY!'

He had yelled, not with anger but with helplessness. The cry of a newborn baby. Sénac beamed.

'Welcome back into the fold, Danny. Your family opens its arms to you in these holiest of hours. In honour of Danny, let us recite the creed.'

I believe in one God, the Father, the Almighty, maker of heaven and earth, of all that is seen and unseen ...

I dreamed that this place was soft. That the walls were soft, that the staircases were soft, that – when colliding with the former or hurtling down the latter, thrown, pushed, exhausted, stumbling – we were met with a warm embrace, a gentle bounce that consoled us and put us back on our feet. I wish I could have told the builders of Saint-Michel-de-Geu to construct it softly.

But, Joe, you will object, be reasonable. Your soft priory would have collapsed. It wouldn't have held firm. There would be nothing there now but a peaceful forest with ancient roots.

Exactly.

Sénac had not invented Oblivion. He had inherited it from his predecessor, Father Puig. The old cellar had been transformed after the war into a 'place of prayer', designed to make uncooperative students understand that, however bad their situation, there was always something worse. Oblivion welcomed all boarders, irrespective of their age. Many of the tears that moistened the concrete were of the purest water and did not fall from any great height. Generally, people stayed there only a day or two, in a darkness barely altered by the sliver of light that crept under the door. The stubbornest sinners would stay there a week at most.

Danny had spent 238 days in that place.

He had been found at the foot of the rock face he had attempted to climb when he was running away. He had sprained his ankle. When he entered Oblivion at the end of April, Danny had sworn he would never apologise. Sénac had promised he would not come out again until he did. *Two hundred and thirty-eight days.* I had lived at Les Confins all that time, never suspecting that a human heart was beating beneath my feet. While I had been jumping on a bed at Henri Fournier's house, shouting the lyrics to 'Sympathy for the Devil' Danny was already in Oblivion. He had been in Oblivion when the Caravelle exploded, when Michael Collins deposited Armstrong and Aldrin on the moon. He had been in Oblivion when I had met Rose, when I had first heard the rhythm, only to lose it again straight away. But that wasn't the most surprising thing.

The most surprising thing was that my friends hadn't lied. Danny was dead.

*

True, his body could still move. Stimulus, reaction: he functioned like an old mechanical piano. The Danny of legend – the legend that the members of The Lookout had forged day after day, that they had relayed to me in the hope that I in turn would embellish it and pass it on to others – that Danny had disappeared months earlier, beaten to a pulp in a flowered dress. As poorly educated and ignorant as they were, my friends had understood, with extraordinary acuity, that he had died that night in spring. It was almost as if they had seen him rise up out of his body, leaving that cumbersome carcass behind on the cold flagstones of Les Confins. Danny no longer existed – they had known that for a long time. And the rest of the orphanage had the proof of it too when, during the first week after his return, he approached a group of three big boys who were shining the shoes of some little kid with their gobs of spit. The bullies froze when they saw him coming – in times past, he would have given them a good hiding – but Danny walked past without even a second glance at the little martyr.

The members of The Lookout were morose. Their former leader had not come to our first meeting after his release. We had defended ourselves from Russian missiles without conviction, before summoning a little more enthusiasm to consult our one-page encyclopaedia in an attempt to understand what the clitoris was for. And when Danny did appear, after everyone else, on the rooftop the following Sunday, their faces fell. I quickly realised that the others resented him because he had sworn he would never apologise. Because he'd had time to whisper, before entering his cell: 'We'll never see each other again,' and Danny never lied. He was fat Elvis now, Schumann at the asylum, Schubert shivering with syphilis, Beethoven conducting his own symphonies out of time because he could not hear the orchestra. He was the senile Haydn, the drunken Sibelius, the toothless

Chet Baker. The version of himself that nobody wanted to see any more, that they wanted to erase from their memory so they could recall only the glory years.

In those early days of 1970, Danny spoke his first words since emerging from the basement. He was sitting against the low wall of the terrace, on a pile of snow, having not bothered to clear it out of the way. We were in the middle of the terrace, ill at ease, gathered around our radio. The old Telefunken was struggling to filter our favourite show through a magnetic storm.

'Who are these wankers?'

His voice was quite ordinary. Neither deep nor high-pitched, just a normal voice, if slightly hoarse. The only unusual thing about it was the fact of its existence after a silence of 238 days.

'Are you deaf? I said who are these wankers?'

'Two new members of The Lookout,' Weasel explained. 'This is Joe and that's Momo.'

'Yeah, I don't think so. I didn't vote on it. All admissions have to be agreed unanimously, and I vote against.'

'Yeah, me too, I vote against it,' said Sinatra.

'Nobody asked you,' Danny replied coldly.

Edison snorted. Sinatra blushed, then gave Danny the finger while he wasn't looking. Weasel kept his cool, as only someone can who, at the age of five, went from the sixth floor to the ground floor in less than two seconds.

'You couldn't vote. You weren't supposed to come back. They've been admitted and that's that.'

Danny capitulated with a shrug. The others resented him even more than before.

One day, when it was sleeting outside, I was climbing the marble steps to the priest's office when I saw Danny coming down the other way. He kept coming to Lookout meetings and not saying anything, and the only trace of life in his motionless body, as he sat there withdrawn, was the blue mist that haloed his lips. He kept his mouth shut as he watched our games with the sardonic detachment of someone who no longer believes in them, but who would give anything to believe again.

He stretched out his leg as I was passing. I fell, face first, onto the steps. I was winded, the taste of blood and stone in my throat. Danny went on his way as if nothing had happened. Then there was the time when he pulled my chair away just as I was about to sit down, and the compass that he stabbed into my hand. I stopped going to Lookout meetings. Momo, naturally, imitated me. Weasel, Edison and Souzix begged us to come back; Sinatra was indifferent. The Lookout returned to its old life, without us, with its patched-up hero back in place. Danny's hostility towards me continued, however, vicious and unexpected. Day by day, that monster from under the ground stole from me the little joy that I had managed to salvage, to clean and to save, from the river of mud that had swept me away one night in May.

On 1 February, Les Confins was buried beneath a legendary snowfall. Everything turned white, beautiful, unrecognisable. The snow slowed our movements, our hearts, our hate. The only exception to this was the hate that Rose and I felt for each other, the radioactive, nuclear hate that united us every Saturday, that radiant globe against which the cold was powerless. It kept me warm all winter.

One morning, Toad came to the classroom to fetch Sinatra. Our friend reappeared an hour later, proudly showing off the red mark in the hollow of his elbow. An American doctor — accompanied by a nurse so beautiful that Sinatra still looked in shock — had come to take his blood. They had advised him to be patient: the results could take time. Apparently Frank was taking the case seriously. He did not want to get it wrong.

On the evening of Candlemas — if I remember correctly, that was what they called pancake day, although there weren't any pancakes — I went out into the courtyard after finishing the priest's correspondence. A weight hit me from above and sent me sprawling in the snow. Blows rained down on my shoulders, my belly, and I saw Danny's face in the light from the front steps, his eyes cold and indifferent. His sudden violence entered my veins, and I was like generations of orphans before me, scratched, bruised, slapped, mouth filled with blood and gravel. While making no attempt to defend myself from his punches, I closed my hands around his neck. This move took him by surprise and, trying to escape my grip, he fell backwards. I held on tight to his throat. His head banged against a step. I kept squeezing. I felt no emotion at all.

Everything dries up in prison — heart, soul, everything but strength, which grows. Danny was tough. He could have fought back. But he loosened his fists and let me strangle him, his mouth open to the air it could no longer breathe. His eyes were calm, almost happy. They were so gentle that I suddenly let go. Danny was staring at the sky, his lips drawn back. Silence, then a gasp, a lurch forward, and he took a massive bite out of the night. He breathed again.

I stood up first, and I made him a promise:

'One day, I'll kill you.'

Danny turned to face me, snowflakes threading his long lashes like pearls.

'Thank you.'

It all began in England, in 2003. In Sheffield, to be precise. And, more precisely still, on Sharrow Vale Road. One day in June – the exact date has been forgotten, but I like to imagine that it was in June – one of the residents left a piano out in the street because he hadn't been able to get it up the stairs of his new apartment. He covered it with a tarp and left a note on it inviting any passer-by who felt like it to play the piano. Public pianos were born that day. Or, at least, the idea we have of a public piano was born: an instrument located at a transport hub, an instrument that belongs to everyone and no one.

But a piano does not need to be in the street, in an airport, in a train station; a piano does not need to be *outside* for it to be public. An open door is enough. The proof? It was through the open door of a musical instruments shop in New York – at 211 W. 58th Street – that a man heard me playing in September 1981. We were in full Indian summer, a season that only America can produce, an afternoon of playful pink shadows that would escape when you weren't looking. The man entered without taking off his hat, a wool trilby. He was tall and the woman with him was beautiful, brilliant and completely insane. (I would discover later that her name was Pannonica and she had a hundred and twenty cats; I still don't know which of these two facts I find the most surprising.) He came over to the piano, which I was trying out for a friend. Our conversation was brief, or I thought so anyway; I was told later that he'd been very talkative. The man put a hand on my shoulder. He hissed slightly when he spoke.

'Your old man teach you to play?' he asked in English.

'Oh, no,' I replied, 'I'm an orphan.'

'You play like that, you ain't an orphan no more.'

Then he left, and the woman smiled at me and followed him.

Thelonious Monk died a few months later. I saw the story in the papers. The man was a genius of jazz, and people had said he was crazy. The public, his colleagues. Crazy because he would sometimes walk off in the middle of a concert, or fall asleep at his keyboard. Crazy for his phrasing, his two-note chords that were no longer chords, his strange hats, his vacant stare and long absences. Crazy because, on the day of his death, he – the genius, the virtuoso – had not touched a piano for six years. Many believe that he had turned away from it.

I know now that he never stopped playing. It was simply that he no longer needed a keyboard.

It was perhaps my fight with Danny, the fear I had felt when I realised I could kill a man – even if the man in question wanted to die – that changed everything. After twenty-four Saturdays, twenty-four hours wasted waiting for Rose to let me in, an entire day of my short life lost on a bench in a dark corridor, facing flowers that had been dead for two hundred years, I'd had enough. On 7 February 1970, I went straight into the reception room without waiting. I expected to find Rose in there, reading a book until the hour was up.

The room was empty. The whispers of the wood panelling, the creaking shadows, everything there breathed the same message: *you do not belong here*. I hastily turned back, but went into the wrong corridor. I tried another door and became completely lost. The house's breathing was stronger now, the audible panting sound – *ahha, ahha* – of a drowsing beast. A voice made me jump, its echoes reverberating through the labyrinth. *Ahha, ahha*. I followed the sound up to a half-open door. The breathing came from there.

Peeking through the gap, I guessed it was a bedroom. A bouquet of wild flowers – real ones this time – made a vain attempt to brighten the interior, but was incapable of dissipating the deathly sadness exhaled by the walls, the memory of the dowagers who had lived there. The grey man I had once glimpsed in the corridor, a few months before, was standing close to a mythological creature, half-woman, half-elephant: Rose, dressed in an old pair of trousers, her small breasts covered only by a bra. She wore a mask over her face and she was connected by a trunk to a strange machine, a sort of bellows inside a metal frame which went up and down, while the man, stethoscope around his neck, took measurements and listened to her chest from time to time.

Rose was trying, her forehead white and glazed with sweat, to work the bellows with the power of her breath alone. I found myself holding my breath and exhaling at the same time as her, because she had not been making me wait for no reason. She was ill. And convalescents have to help each other.

I had seen that device once before at our family doctor's. *Tuberculosis*. My hate started to crack. I tried desperately to keep it whole, to stop it breaking apart, but it was too late. It was fracturing like Weasel's bedroom one Christmas Eve, huge slabs were falling from it, shattering into toxic sand, the pipes were sagging and water was spurting out of them, sweeping away everything in its path as the entire thing collapsed and died. I did what any reasonable man would have done: I ran away.

The governess found me sitting on the front steps, shivering in the wool coat that we orphans were given for the winter. She wasn't happy – 'I was looking everywhere for you' – and I followed her furious trot into the reception room. Rose, at the piano, was now wearing a cream-coloured dress in textured silk with four black buttons arranged in a square – two at the shoulders, two beneath the chest. Marc Bohan again. I think I can say that, like Thelonious Monk, Marc Bohan had found the rhythm. A rhythm of needles and swansdown, perhaps, but a rhythm all the same.

'You're late,' she observed. 'I do have other things to do, you know.'

'No, you don't.'

During the thirty minutes I had spent out in the cold, I had managed to rebuild my hate, or rather I had constructed a containment system for it, a patch-up job that would hold it in place for the duration of the lesson. Back at the orphanage, I would have a week to build something more solid, to consolidate and secure it. As for Rose, her hate was completely intact. It was made from pure marble, and not just any marble: the Italian marble of the Borgias and the Medici. But something in the chemistry of the air – in the subtle equilibrium that controlled the permanent collision of our rages – changed that day in February.

Rose stood up and stopped a few feet in front of me, imperious.

'You have no right to speak to me like that.'

'I'll talk to you how I—'

She slapped me, gracefully. She started to turn back to the piano, but I grabbed her arm. Rose coldly freed herself.

'Don't touch me!'

'Or what?'

'Or I'll scream rape.'

'Who'd want to rape a consumptive?'

In 1908, in Siberia, a shock wave of mysterious origin flattened the earth, knocking down sixty thousand trees, blowing away everything in its path for a hundred kilometres around. It sent a vortex of dust and ash as far away as Spain. No impact crater was ever discovered. The most recent scientific explanations attribute the phenomenon to the explosion of a meteor less than ten kilometres from the earth. I know that to be untrue. What really happened is that a man, somewhere on the banks of the Tunguska river, offended a woman.

'Who told you that?' she asked in a barely audible voice.

'I … I saw it. By accident! I was looking for this room and I got lost and—'

'Shut up.'

She was about to call her father. Have me thrown out. The count would tell Toad everything, and the chief monitor, perhaps surprised to realise I was such a vicious, nasty child, would give me a congratulatory pat on the back before handing me over to the priest.

Rose went back to the piano and sat down.

'I'm glad I didn't post your letter,' she said at last.

'You didn't post our letter?'

'No.'

'Why not?'

'I read it.'

'*What?*'

'I didn't think it would be good for Papa, who has given you so much, if there was a scandal,' she explained. 'Anyway, so now we're quits. Let's play.'

Dumbstruck, furious – although with whom, I wasn't sure – I sat down beside her. She opened the score. Beethoven's Sonata no. 1, a youthful work in which Ludwig had disguised himself as Mozart. But his vigorous, powerful body – not yet suffering from its future torments of genius and deafness (and who is to say that the latter was worse than the former?) – burst the seams of the costume he wore. I sight-read the music mechanically. After a few bars, Rose closed the piano lid. I just had time to pull my fingers away.

'I'm not a consumptive. I *had* consumption. Almost a year ago. The antibiotics worked – I'm cured. But I still suffer from shortness of breath, the doctors don't know why. They say I need fresh air. That's why we're here. I have to do breathing exercises to regain full lung capacity. Are you happy now?'

'I didn't want to—'

'Yes, you did. You wanted to know. Or to hurt me. Same thing.'

'You didn't need to hide the fact that you were … that you used to be ill.'

'I didn't hide anything. It was right there, in front of you. Can't you hear the way I breathe?'

She was about to slump down on the sofa where she usually read her book.

'What is The Lookout? That thing you talk about in the letter?'

'A secret society.'

She started to laugh, with a sparkle I had never heard in her before.

'It's not secret any more, though, is it? Seeing as you just talked about it! And what's the point of this secret society?'

'Nothing.'

'Why does it exist then?'

I shrugged. 'To do something pointless.'

She nodded and began playing with her book, though she didn't open it.

'I'm sorry. I'll post your letter, I promise.'

'Doesn't matter. It won't change anything anyway.'

'I'm still going to post it though.'

Then she tossed her book to me. *The Lives of the Great Saints.*

'I pretend to read that, for my parents. It's so boring ... Do you know any stories?'

'Some sad stories. We had a contest.'

'Tell me.'

'Aren't we supposed to be playing the piano?'

'If anyone asks, we can just say you were teaching me to read music.'

Rose patted the empty space beside her on the sofa.

'Tell me,' she repeated. 'And you'd better not bore me.'

I told her about Sinatra, Weasel, Edison, Souzix, the way the light had a thousand different ways of going out. I told her about Danny, because his were the only stories I had left. The others had burned up in a breath of jet fuel. Leaning back on the armrest, one slender finger on the bridge of her nose, Rose listened, her face serious.

'Not bad,' she said finally. 'I know a sad story too. Sadder than all yours put together. It begins like this: "Once upon a time there was a young bullfighter." Do you want to hear it?'

And, like an idiot, I said yes.

Once upon a time there was a young bullfighter. This was in Seville, at the start of the Spanish Civil War. Everyone agreed he was talented, that he killed like no man alive, like Death himself. But the war reduced the number of corridas, and the bullfighter spent his life trying to find the fiercest, most dangerous *toro*, the animal that would make his name in a single afternoon.

The bullfighter had a wife, a very beautiful and very sweet woman. He loved her more than anything, except perhaps the *muleta*, the red cloth that he waved at bulls. 'You don't need the bullring,' she told him. 'You don't need your fancy clothes. You don't need anything, because you have me and I have you.' The bullfighter replied: 'I want to cover you with jewels, dress you in light, like me. I will be the equal of that boy, Manolete, the talk of Madrid. I will bathe in sand, I will bathe in blood, I will come back famous, and you will be famous too.'

The war continued, and the young woman became gravely ill with consumption. The bullfighter did not have much money, particularly since he spent his days scouring the country in search of a worthy adversary. But he had friends, who collected enough money to send his wife to the mountains for treatment. The bullfighter remained in Seville. Two months passed and he heard very little news of his wife, the war having cut most lines of communication. One day, a message reached him from the Granada area. A breeder had heard about the bullfighter's search, and he believed he had the animal he was looking for.

The bullfighter immediately set off. When he arrived, his eye was caught by a young bull pacing around an enclosure. The bull was completely white – something that the bullfighter had never seen before. As soon as the bullfighter approached it, his face lit up with wonder, the animal charged, head down, at the barrier that separated them, almost smashing a hole in it. The bullfighter had found his adversary.

He went home and put his house up for sale to fund the purchase of the bull, which he wanted to fight when it became an adult. Soon afterwards, a letter arrived, the page half torn. It had been sent two weeks before. His wife had died, far away in the mountains. The bullfighter wept for a long time and bitterly reproached himself for his vanity, which had separated him from the woman he loved more than anything in the world, except perhaps the *muleta*. His friends tried to console him; they urged him to think about the future, to prepare for the combat of his life. So the bullfighter waited, four long years. He got married again – to a woman from the village whom he had known long before. The *novillo* grew and became a *toro*. All of Seville clamoured to see the white bull in action – until then, it had been kept away from the bullring. As soon as it emerged from the bullpen, as soon as it saw its matador, the animal charged at him. The bullfighter made a few passes, sizing up this strange adversary that stopped in surprise each time he evaded it. On the second *tercio*, the matador planted three pairs of banderillas in the creature's back. And the beautiful white fur, already dimmed by dust, was now stained crimson. Again and again the bull attacked, refusing to be distanced, moving closer and closer, complicating the bullfighter's ability to make passes. The matador, though, had not worked for four years in vain. And when the exhausted animal advanced, head lowered, at the end of the *faena*, the bullfighter let its horns touch his chest, to the cheers of the crowd. Then he delivered the *estocada*. The white bull fell to its knees and, even then, one last time, shoved its muzzle against the man's calves, refusing defeat. The crowd, hysterical, carried the bullfighter across town. This legendary fight made him rich and famous. He worked for a long time and retired, undefeated, at the age of seventy, to spend his time with his wife, his children and his grandchildren. And when he looked back over his life, his only regret was that he had not been with the woman he loved more than anything in the world – perhaps even more than the *muleta*, he was starting to think now – when she had died on a faraway mountain.

He was eighty, and aware that his days were numbered, when a letter arrived. It was a letter from the depths of the past, the paper stiff and yellow, the postmark dated 1940, that had been found wedged behind a sorting rack during the renovation of a post office in Madrid. A letter that his wife had written to him from her sanatorium in Switzerland, which said:

> *I do not have much strength left. I know now that I am going to leave this world. Don't be sad. Last night, I had a dream. You know my grandmother was something of a witch, and that I believe in those things. In this dream, my grandmother told me I was not going to die, not really, that I would now live in a different form: a bull, but a bull very different from other bulls. A completely white bull. So, if our paths ever cross again, my love, do not be surprised, one day, to see a great white bull running towards you.*

'So?' Rose asked.

So I kissed her.

'Did you slip her your tongue?'

As soon as I returned, my friends guessed. Seeing my red cheeks and my confused gaze, they knew that something had happened. I confessed everything. How I had bent Rose backwards in my arms, Rhett Butler-style, how I had ravished her with a long kiss. How I had laid her on the sofa, because her legs were too weak to hold her up now I had stolen away her breath with my passion. She had barely found the strength to whisper 'Again'. As for the tongue, that was none of their business. Besides, at Les Confins, nobody was really interested in the truth.

Thankfully. In fact, it happened like this ...

'So?' Rose asked.

So I kissed her.

She shoved me brusquely away and slapped me for the second time that day.

'What's wrong with you? Who do you think you are?'

Then she kissed me, with all her strength. That was how I discovered that women are complicated. Thérèse von Brunswick, Giulietta Guicciardi, Anna Margarete von Browne, Antonie Brentano ... It was hardly surprising that Beethoven, who wasn't simple either, had dedicated his works to them.

'Do you think I'm beautiful, Joseph?'

'Well, yeah.'

'"Well, yeah"? What are you, a caveman? Didn't you ever learn how to speak to a woman?'

'Yes, I think you're beautiful.'

'Beautiful how?'

'Like C minor.'

C minor was Beethoven's favourite key. The sound of beauty prowling in a storm. One could not exist without the other. Rose stared at me, speechless.

'That's what my old music teacher used to tell his wife. That she was beautiful like C minor.'

'And is she? Beautiful?'

I thought about Mina, in her too-large clothes, her arms buried up to the elbows in washing-up or in the arse of a goose she'd just plucked. I thought about that queen faded by life, wind, light. No, she wasn't beautiful, not in the way Rose meant.

'She's magnificent.'

Rose melted into my embrace. I had just learned how to speak to a woman.

Winter 1970. Five Saturdays. Five long sighs amid our cacophony. As soon as the governess left us, Rose and I would move closer together on the piano bench, and nervously pretend to play. Our hands brushed on the keyboard, then scurried away like frightened spiders, she towards the high notes, me towards the low, before finding each other again in the middle.

At night, in Les Confins, I told the others everything. I lied like crazy, turning myself into a Casanova, but I lied without lying because, really, what did it matter how hesitant or clumsy we were? The essential part was true. My friends didn't need to know that she had slipped me her tongue first, that I'd been so startled I jumped back like an idiot. They didn't need to know that, when I'd put a hand on her right breast, she had slapped me again before grabbing my hand and putting it back in the same place. My classmates listened, rapt, applauded my exploits. Only Danny sniggered in his corner but said nothing. Except once, to ask what Rose wore. The others stared at him strangely, and he didn't speak again after that.

Thanks to Souzix, I almost blew it. He wanted to know if I was going to marry Rose, and I laughed in his face. During my next visit to the house, though, after one particularly glorious kiss, I whispered:

'You think we'll get married one day?'

'Certainly not. Don't be so bourgeois.'

'Me, bourgeois? I sleep in the same room as forty snoring boys!'

'The bourgeoisie is a mental thing.'

Deeply upset, I shrugged, feigning indifference.

'You're right. Besides, we hardly know each other.'

'That's not true, Joseph. We knew everything about each other from our first meeting, but we forgot it. Now we are spending our time rediscovering it.'

She spoke like Rothenberg. I didn't know whether to laugh or cry.

'But I will never get married. Not to you or to anyone else. It's nothing personal.'

'Why?'

'That's just how it is. Are we talking or kissing?'

We were kissing. A lot. Although we did make sure we played a few distracted chords from time to time. My good mood spread like a virus through the rest of the orphanage. Kids started smiling for no reason, infected by the invisible joy that floated through the air. Even Toad began whistling while he patrolled outside the showers, staring at certain boys, making sarcastic or admiring comments on how well or otherwise nature had endowed us, delighting us with multiple slang words for homosexuals.

One night in March, Sénac announced during dinner that there would be a big surprise at the end of that week. The surprise turned out to be the delivery of a brand-new metal sign bearing the words: *Departmental Directorate of Sanitary and Social Affairs – Les Confins*. It was to replace the worm-eaten wooden arrow nailed to a post and pointing at the ground, which said simply:

Orphanage. There was talk of inviting the regional deputy to inaugurate the new sign, but apparently he was not available. The prefect was discussed, then the local education officer, then the mayor. Nobody came, and in the end Toad installed the sign himself. When I say 'himself', what I mean is that he stood smoking and watched as the four chosen orphans, including Edison and Souzix, dug two holes, wasted two hundred kilos of concrete that Toad decided was too lumpy, remade another two hundred kilos that he grumblingly approved, and finished the job. Sénac gathered everyone around the sign, shook a sprinkler of holy water, and spent a long time contemplating this new arrival, his eyes wet with emotion.

I didn't care about any of that. Every Saturday, I kissed Rose. When we weren't kissing, she made me talk. She wanted to know everything about me, everything I'd ever seen and felt. She questioned me constantly about my parents' plane crash, as if she envied me. I refused to respond. The following Saturday, she insisted. I owed her the fire, the gold, the alchemical mysteries. She was demanding. But she paid me well, with a flutter of her eyelids.

I kissed Rose and we told each other: 'Everything will be okay.' That was the only future we dared discuss.

Rothenberg spotted the piano as soon as he left the concert hall, like an eagle spotting a mouse. A myopic and tearful eagle, maybe, but an eagle all the same. The instrument was separated from the lobby by a velvet rope which was in the process of being installed or removed. A sign ordered onlookers not to touch it.

It was the interval. My teacher had brought me to the Salle Pleyel to listen to a young prodigy whose name I have forgotten. The pianist had massacred Rothenberg's favourite sonata – no. 29, 'Hammerklavier'. Mina was with us, her head just sticking up out of a fake-fur coat. While she went to buy a beer, Rothenberg pulled me by the sleeve, walked past the rope and sat down at the piano. He kicked the sign away.

'I don't think we're allowed, Monsieur Rothenberg ...'

'Oh, and that guy we just heard *is* allowed? He plays like a boxer. And not Muhammad Ali either. A *bad* boxer. An elephant. Did you hear the first chords? He plays like this ...'

He hammered the piano, making half of the audience members at the bar jump off their seats, then turned to me.

'But Monsieur Rothenberg ...'

'Yes, Monsieur Marty?'

'The sonata is called "Hammerklavier".'

'So?'

'So aren't you *supposed* to hammer the keys?'

Rothenberg slapped his own forehead.

'*Oy vey*. *Hammerklavier* is just the German word for a pianoforte. It's an invitation to play an instrument with strings that are struck rather than plucked. *Do not play my music on a harpsichord*, Ludwig is telling us, *but on a piano*. It is not an invitation to beat the hell out of the instrument! Listen, this is the Adagio – does it make you want to beat someone up? You see any hammers?'

He played and silence fell around me, it fell upon the people at the bar, it fell on the Rue du Faubourg-Saint-Honoré. Silence probably fell on Alpha Centauri, if there was any noise there in the first place. He played the entire Adagio, forgetting the Pleyel, with syncopated softness. And he did what he rarely did: he spoke to me at the same time.

'Do you want to play like this one day, my little Joe?'

'Yes, Monsieur Rothenberg.'

'Then you must hear, *bubele*. Hear the voice of your people.'

'I'm not Jewish, Monsieur Rothenberg.'

He laughed.

'No, of course you're not Jewish. You're much too stupid to be Jewish. But you are human, right? Even if I do wonder sometimes.'

All the spectators had gathered around him. Make-up was running down the women's faces. Men who, all week long, had murdered and crucified people, now had to pretend they had a speck of dust in their eye.

'Lean close, *bubele*,' the old leopard whispered. 'Don't spoil the music for them by talking too loud. That's it, like that. I won't always be here, you know.'

'Oh, Monsieur Rothenberg ...'

'Shut up. When I'm not there any more, if you're not sure how to play a sonata, listen to Kempff. He's the greatest. Even when he gets it wrong, he's right.'

'I don't understand, Monsieur Rothenberg.'

'Because you don't hear. Beethoven was completely deaf when he wrote this piece. But he *heard*. What I'm playing – and I'm playing one of the most beautiful adagios in history: look at their faces if you don't believe me – what I'm playing for you, I'm not searching inside myself for it. Inside, I'm old, sick. Inside, I'm empty – other men have made sure of that. Inside, I'm dirty. To play like this, you have to get a taste of the outside. You have to find the rhythm.'

The last notes faded slowly. A choked silence. Someone shouted 'Bravo!' The applause drowned out the bell calling spectators back to their seats. Standing close to her husband, Mina was beaming. An emotion that almost looked like happiness smoothed the wrinkles of my old teacher's face. Not for long, just a second. The audience demanded an encore, which he played. Then another one after that. The concert hall director asked Rothenberg to stop and was booed by the crowd. Their anger grew and when the director turned away his hair was dishevelled, his bow tie askew.

And so he did what anyone does, in this earthly existence, when they see beauty prowling on a dark night. He called the police.

That Saturday, two weeks before Easter, I sensed instantly that something was wrong. Rose was waiting for me at the piano, in a green dress, looking tense. Dior must be worn with nonchalance, my mother always told me, and I passed this advice on to Rose.

'It's not Dior,' she replied coldly. 'It's Balenciaga.'

She seemed angry, and yet I hadn't done anything. I had not yet acquired the wisdom that comes with age and allows men to understand that women are like the Church. To understand that you have sinned, whether in thought or word or action or omission, and that you must beg forgiveness even if you haven't done anything, because there is no sense in arguing against a divine decree. On the keyboard, her hands fled mine. When I leaned towards her, lips puckered, she recoiled.

'We shouldn't have, Joseph.'

'Huh?'

'Where is it going, all this? Nowhere. You know it as well as I do.'

'Yes. I understand.'

'You understand? You're not angry? I tell you it's over and you *understand*?'

'A girl as beautiful as you, with someone as … I understand.'

Finally she took pity on me, with my eternal beaten-dog whimper, and placed a hand on my cheek.

'Sorry. I was hoping we'd fight. That would have been easier. My father called yesterday. We're going back to Paris.'

'So you don't think I'm ugly?'

'Of course I don't. I think you're handsome, especially when you play the piano. Even if you've never played it again like you did that first time.'

'I will. I promise. As soon as I understand how I did it.'

'Didn't you hear what I said? I'm going back to Paris next week. It's over. We won't see each other again.'

For the first time since 2 May 1969 at 6:14 p.m., everything seemed clear to me.

'It's not over.'

'What do you mean?'

'Whereabouts in Paris do you live?'

'Rue de Passy, why?'

'I'm going to run away. I'm going to leave Les Confins. I'll find you.'

'Don't be ridiculous. You're not going to run away.'

'Aren't I? We'll see about that.'

I left the room. Practically sprinting. Rose caught up with me in the corridor, in front of the herbarium, still withering within its dark frames.

'Are you *really* going to run away?'

'Yes.'

'I'll go with you then.'

I stared at her, dumbstruck. Rose, with her beautiful dresses and her porcelain skin.

'I know what you're thinking, Joseph. You're wrong. I've been thinking about leaving for a long time. You really think I want to turn into my mother?'

I shrugged. 'I don't know your mother.'

'There's nothing to know. She doesn't exist. She's a good little wife. Why do you think my father spends his weeks in Paris? He's got girlfriends there. Why do you think they want me to learn the piano? So that, one day, I will become one too – a good little wife, who never makes any trouble and who knows how to welcome clients, colleagues, financial backers. The kind of wife who keeps a list of all her menus in a little notebook so she never embarrasses herself by serving the same meal twice to the same guest. That's why they're hiding me here, until I'm fully cured. Being a former consumptive is *definitely* not the kind of thing men want in a good little wife. You think that's the life I dream about?'

'What do you dream about?'

Travelling. She wanted to see Inca palaces in the rain, chew bitter mushrooms that would transform her into an eagle, a wolf, a weasel, bite into frosted lemons one morning in Sicily, pull a face and spit it all out, set fire to her lungs with the air from an ice floe, offer her pale throat to the mouth of a volcano. She had heard that when certain men sang, two voices came out of the same mouth. She wanted to become a diplomat, just in case those Vietnamese people bombed, machine-gunned and burned with flamethrowers by Toad in his songs might, by chance, want to tell their side of the story. She thought it was wiser to get along, to come to an agreement – *you scratch my back, a bit higher, to the left, and I'll scratch yours* – and that everyone would be happy once their itches had been scratched. She thought that those who waved a flag and imagined it unique were all waving the same thing. She said all this, and I so desperately wanted to believe her, even if I had never heard of a female diplomat before.

'I'm going with you, Joseph. And just to be clear: I'm not asking your permission.'

'It's too risky.'

'I told you, I've been thinking about this for a long time. I have a plan.'

For several months, she had secretly been learning to drive. She had convinced the new gardener to teach her, when her parents weren't there. And they often weren't there, thanks to her father's girlfriends and her mother's good deeds. The gardener felt affectionate – perhaps more than that – towards the 'young lady who seemed so bored', the girl with no sparkle in her eyes. Rose was a diligent driver, she just found it quite difficult to get out of first gear. The plan was simple: she would leave around midnight, when her mother was asleep, numbed by Valium. After I had escaped, I would just have to meet her. She would wait for me on the wide bend in the road, about thirty minutes' walk from Les Confins. By daybreak, we would be far, far away.

'Far away where?'

'Spain.'

'They'll stop us at the border.'

Rose laughed.

'The border is for idiots. My mother's from there, we spend all our holidays there. I know a way. I've checked it on a map.'

'What will we do in Spain?'

'We'll work, until we're old enough to do what we want. I'll take some money from Maman's purse, but we'll still need to earn a living. Afterwards, I'll go to university there and I'll become a diplomat. You'll play the piano. In bars, to start with, and then one day a talent scout will spot you and you'll become a world-famous star.'

'Do you speak Spanish?'

'Not a word. We'll learn. A diplomat has to speak several languages anyway.'

'It'll never work. You're dreaming.'

'Yes, Joseph. I'm dreaming. I'm sixteen.'

'I can't see your plan working. It's improbable.'

'It's improbable that a plane should crash.'

I thought she was going to apologise. But Rose did not apologise. She turned to the wall, searching the darkness for a painting. Her fingers found a dazzling flower, a whirl of ivory and gold on a corolla of fire.

'The *Selenicereus*. My favourite flower. We're like the *Selenicereus*, you and me. We bloom in the dark.'

She was right: I should have heard her breathing. An orphan's breathing, hollow and penumbral, which – hemmed in too tightly – ended up consuming the one it was supposed to bring to life. She was one of us. Spirit me away, spirit her away, spirit us away. Talking about Rose and saying *us*!

'We could go to Vegas one day ... I might know someone there.'

'If you like. But what do you mean you *might* know someone there?'

'It's complicated. I'll leave tomorrow night, after the Lookout meeting. I have to tell them.'

'No, my father will be here tomorrow night. Monday. One last thing ...'

'Yeah?'

'I will never be a good little wife. I'm not leaving for you. I'm leaving *with* you.'

She accompanied me to the door. In the darkness, I shivered when she took my hand. A black rain was riddling the earth, smashing the leaves and the boldest buds, which had suddenly appeared in profusion at the first hint of spring. On the threshold, Rose clung to my fingers for a second.

'Look, it's raining. Do you think it's your fault, Joseph?'

'My fault? No, that's ridiculous.'

'So you're not the reason it's raining.'

'Of course not.'

'If you're not the reason it's raining, then you're also not the reason why aeroplanes fall from the sky.'

They all wanted to stop me. I was crazy. I was going to die. Even Momo looked sad. And then Danny, sitting in his usual spot beside the wall, decided to speak.

'If he wants to leave, let him. At least one of you has a pair of balls.'

'I have balls!' Souzix protested.

'Hairy balls,' Danny said.

Souzix said nothing. Danny stood up, and traced the path of the gutter with his finger, pointing out its weak spots.

'You have to get from the north facade to the east to reach the place where you can jump over the fence. Just follow the gutter. But be careful: down there, where it turns the corner of the building, that's the most dangerous spot. It's come loose. If you put too much weight on it, it'll crack. And you have to put your weight on it to get round the corner.'

'How did you manage?'

'I don't remember.'

'Are you really leaving?' Souzix asked. 'It's not that bad here, is it?'

He was holding back tears. His teeth were gritted so hard, to stop his lips trembling, that the rest of his body was dancing the tarantella. Marie-Ange was talking to us a bit, but tonight all we heard were the interminable silences between the words. Even she seemed weary, exhausted by this live show in the middle of the night, tired of having to support all the damaged people in the world with her voice alone. We turned off the radio, we strolled from Vegas to the Milky Way, we delayed the inevitable as long as we could. The night condensed and froze around us. It was time to go inside.

'I'll write to you.'

'Don't make any promises you won't keep,' said Weasel.

He took my hand.

'Don't forget us. That would be enough.'

It was snowing hard that Monday, a return to winter that threatened to complicate my task. The orphanage was asleep, the sound of its breathing like a single breath. A cold breeze caressed the still bodies, pouring through a little window that Toad had left open – 'and the first kid to close it will have to answer to me'. Weasel, wrapped up warmly under his bed, winked at me and whispered 'Good luck.'

I didn't have any gloves. The burning metal, the night's sharp teeth: all I felt was pain. My breath petrified in blue clouds that hung there, immobile, in front of me, shocked by the cold air. The old building creaked, and so did everything else: the ice on the nearby mountain, the gutter. The gutter creaked loudest of all, its entire length protesting when I hung from it. The building was four storeys high. It took me ten minutes to descend the few metres separating me from the third floor, my head floating in the cotton-wool clouds that I exhaled ever faster, my lungs on fire, my muscles paralysed by the effort. My legs got tangled up in my woollen coat. I paused in front of a window with open shutters, revealing a room I had never seen before. The moonlight illuminated a cemetery of toys – teddy bears with forgotten names, trains whose wooden wheels would never take them anywhere – presumably all confiscated when the boarders arrived. Momo had been lucky they'd let him keep Asinus. A bear with a torn ear gazed at me imploringly. I ignored it and continued my descent. *Every man for himself*.

Halfway there. Beneath my feet, a cornice the width of a

hand, glossy with fresh ice in places. Below that, ten metres of nothingness, then the sharp, pointed posts of the rusted fence that ran alongside the building. Behind that fence was a dead end: a cliff face rising a hundred metres up in the air.

Calm down, son. You're using up too much oxygen.

Is that you, Michael Collins? I know men aren't supposed to say this sort of thing to each other, but I'm really happy to hear your voice. I haven't talked to you much recently, because I made some friends. I'm sorry. They'd have thought I was crazy.

Did you think I'd abandon you? Just when you were about to return to the earth? Keep your eyes on the prize, son. An astronaut never panics. He analyses a problem then solves it.

Clinging to the wall, to that stone worn smooth by years of storms, I was getting closer to the corner. The gutter hung loose, its fastening broken just at that spot. Danny was right: there was no way I could rely on it to get me around to the other side of the building. A velvet breath caressed my cheek and I almost let go. An eagle owl flew away, unruffled, perhaps having thought that any creature that high up, in its domain, must be another owl. *Analyse the problem.* Danny had made it. The wind grew stronger, scratching at the rendered wall. Leaning forward, I finally managed to see the two holes in the wall, half filled with snow, on the eastern facade. I could slip the thumb and index finger of my left hand quite deeply into those holes. And, holding on with just those two digits, climb around the corner.

The left hand, of course. The rhythm hand, the one on which everything depends, as in Sonata no. 15, which Rothenberg loved so much. It was a musical movement, an act of creation. Thumb, index finger. Abandoning the body. Two digits versus the void. My legs were shaking. Two digits versus a fall. My left foot moved from the gutter to the cornice on the eastern facade. Two digits versus a broken neck or – worse – impalement on a fence post. I was straddling the building's angle now, one foot on either side, and Les Confins pushed against my chest with that cold stone ridge, as if trying to slice me in two. This was the moment. I let go of everything, except for those two digits, and reassembled myself on the other side of the gutter. I had made it.

That was when I saw Toad. Just below my feet, five metres away. He was smoking and humming a tune – he hadn't noticed me. My right foot slipped. I let it slip, anchored to the facade by my two digits and my left foot. A small pile of fresh snow came loose from the cornice and fell, twirling, towards Toad, disintegrating miraculously in a gust of wind before reaching his head. The monitor stubbed out his cigarette, spat a yellow gob on the ground and walked away, hands in his pockets.

My foot, heavy as a piece of wood, found the cornice. On this side of the building, the gutter was more firmly attached. I forced myself to count to a hundred, imagining Toad going to his room – he must be there by now – and then to a hundred again just in case he'd stopped somewhere on the way. I started moving again, as silently as possible. When I reached the point where the fence came close to the orphanage, I pushed off against the wall as hard as I could. I landed three metres below in a snowdrift. Dazed. Free. Somewhere in the ink-black night, the eagle owl raised its great eyebrows, wondering how any creature could fly so badly.

Well done, son. Mission accomplished. Time for me to go home now. If one day you happen to be in Houston, if one day you feel lonely – and it'll happen – knock at my door. My wife and I will be happy to welcome you to our home. We'll talk about the good old days until late at night. We'll talk about the moon, just the two of us, because nobody else has seen the things we've seen.

While I caught my breath, I took one last look at Les Confins. Thirty minutes' walk away, Rose was waiting for me on the wide bend. Here, the courtyard was in darkness, everyone was asleep. I started to run. First, I had to get through the woods – three or four hundred metres of absolute darkness – before I reached the road that led down to the village. I knew the way by heart. There, the tall, bent beech tree. Then the Les Confins sign, firmly fixed upon its smooth concrete feet. Another hundred metres along the dirt path and it would turn to tarmac – and freedom. There would be black ice. I would slow down.

The road appeared. The road, and a car parked at the junction, in the middle of the path, crouching in the darkness. The headlights blinded me. Behind the steering wheel sat the priest, his round face crystallised by cold, a barrier between me and my freedom. Without thinking, I turned the other way, going back into the forest to escape the headlights' beam. A rustling sound followed me, something crawling quickly, a predatory mass that silenced the smaller creatures. Behind me, then on the sides. I turned again, at random. I jumped over a fallen trunk, hurtled down a slope and fell, cutting open my knee, then back on my feet and running again. A stream. I followed it, to put the dogs off the scent. But there were no dogs. I crossed it then, the tree branches scratching my cheeks, clinging to my sleeves. The trees were holding me back, jealous of my freedom, they who would never leave this black valley. Toad surged from behind a pine tree, right in front of me, ablaze with life and joy. He was at home here. Half-man, half-beast, with a rare beauty that Indochina had not understood. I had escaped him in Cao Bang. I had escaped him in Dien Bien Phu. Now, at last, he had me.

With the cowardly relief of the prey, the happiness of being held, I rushed into his arms. Then collapsed, because I didn't want to make things easy for him, into a pile of empty clothes that weighed a ton – Souzix's technique. Toad dragged me effortlessly to the road, delighted to have tricked me so easily, giving me a few kicks along the way.

I hurt, but not where he hit me. My pain was far away from his blows, my pain was deep inside. I thought about Rose, waiting for me, scanning the night in her rear-view mirror, and that was what hurt me. But even further away, even more deeply, I felt a numb pain in my gut.

I had not told anyone but my closest friends that I was leaving. There was a traitor in The Lookout.

I know you won't answer any more. I'm too far away now. I'm recording this message and entrusting it to chance, to the stellar winds, so that you will know what didn't work. You were wrong to have confidence in me. I flunked the final manoeuvre, the most important: the rendezvous. I am sinking into the great indigo, whirling aimlessly under the patient gaze of white dwarfs, red and blue giants. Constellations in my visor, the silk of comets between my gloved hands, I waltz alone on a floor of stars. There is no sound here, only my breathing, the beating of my heart. If someone finds my empty spacesuit, one day in the distant future, at the other end of a nova, he will never suspect that I undertook this crazy voyage for a girl. But you, Michael Collins, I want you to know.

The door of Oblivion banged shut behind me on 16 March 1970. Toad had shaved my head. The priest had forced me to take the penitent's march, a guard of honour in the opposite direction from the one taken by Danny when he was released. I had to shake everyone's hand, even the little ones, and ask them for forgiveness. They all stared at me curiously, except for the boys from The Lookout, who lowered their eyes. When Danny took my hand, he pulled me into a rough embrace and whispered in my ear:

'Welcome to The Lookout.'

Momo wouldn't let go of me. He didn't understand what I was going to do in there. I tried to free myself, I told him in a murmur that everything would be all right, but he just moaned and shook his head ever harder. Toad gave him a massive slap that sent

Asinus flying. Momo ran for his life and went to hide where he thought nobody would find him, deep within himself, in a secret lair of muscle spasms, spit, fingers tensed above the void. Toad carried him out straight away. They weren't about to let some epileptic ostrich spoil the solemnity of the moment.

Before closing the door on me, the priest muttered: 'Psalm 68:6, Joseph: "the rebellious live in a sun-scorched land".'

And the darkness took me.

Rose was right. I was not responsible for my parents' deaths. I felt like I had survived the accident when the truth was that I was the principal victim. The explosion had sent me flying, transforming me into a human missile that soared further and further into outer space. The only way of returning to earth would be ricocheting off something hard.

The priest would come in the middle of the night – at least, I think it was, because night was eternal there – to read me a passage of Holy Scripture. But he always stood on the other side of the door. The only person I saw was Toad, who brought me two meals a day and escorted me once a day to the toilet, an old earthenware bowl secreted in one of the side alcoves. He left the door open as I did my business. Instead of having the decency to turn his back on me, he would stare straight into my eyes. I was constipated for a week. After seven days, straight in the eyes or not, it all came out. I did not yet know that I was being given the luxury treatment.

Sénac knew about every aspect of the plan that I had revealed to The Lookout. Rose had been found parked by the side of the road. She had tried to get away but, unable to shift the car into second gear, had ended up in a ditch fifty metres away, thankfully unhurt. The gendarmes had taken her home, and her father had returned urgently from Paris. The story spread all the way to Lourdes.

'To avoid embarrassment, I informed Rose's family that, when you came back from your last piano lesson, you had come to me and confessed everything. I told them you had let me know all the details of your plan to run away because you already regretted it, and that you had sought my spiritual aid.'

Rose thought I'd abandoned her.

She must have cursed me until she was out of breath. It is perhaps this that I find it hardest to forgive Sénac for, even now. The darkness continued, the silence, the solitude of Adam, that same absolute solitude that Michael Collins had experienced as he flew around the dark side of the moon. I begged the priest to forgive me – abjectly, several times – for what I had done.

'And what did you do?' he asked me through the door.

'I ran away. I disobeyed.'

'That is not your greatest sin.'

Like a good Catholic, I invented as many sins as I could think of. But no matter how hard I tried – confessing imaginary crimes for the pleasure of being forgiven, like a man who takes his car to a car wash every Sunday before driving along muddy paths again on Monday morning – nothing satisfied Sénac. I slept in bursts, I rehearsed scores, I rehearsed rehearsals. I did physical exercises, and I gave up physical exercises. I am not afraid to say that I hated. I hated Sénac, even more than I hated Toad.

I was obsessed by the mysterious traitor. Who had talked? The obvious candidates were Danny, to test me, and Sinatra, who had never liked me much anyway. Then there was Weasel, whose interests always came first. When I was a kid, my grandmother had got me into Agatha Christie. 'If you read only one thing, read Agatha,' she advised me, with the bizarre, muddled chauvinism of the English. In Agatha Christie novels, the culprit was always the one you least suspected. Souzix, because he was weak? Edison, because he had been promised all the maths, physics and chemistry textbooks he had ever dreamed of? *No, no,* Poirot ranted, *you can't see the wood for the trees. The one you least suspect is Rose herself!*

I slowly drove myself mad. Drop by drop, my reason trickled out through my pores, my ears, my eyes. Especially my eyes.

One night, the priest announced:

'I opened the suitcase that you brought here when you arrived.'

I didn't care if he'd opened it. I turned to face the wall, wrapped in a blanket on my rusted bed base. I would have given all the suitcases I'd ever owned to speak to Rose for just a minute, to tell her that I had not betrayed her, that I had never truly hated her, or only in a strange way that made me feel hot under the collar, that I had wanted to kiss her for a long time, since the first fire, since bison had first danced in cave paintings. That suitcase had been packed by our neighbour before my departure for the moon. Madame Desmaret must have shoved in everything she could find in my bedroom. I had hardly used it at all, since I had been given clothes wherever I went. All I had ever taken from it were a few sweaters and my toiletries.

'At the bottom of your suitcase, I found a record.'

I opened my eyes. The priest was fiddling with something – putting on his reading glasses. I put my ear to the door.

'"Sympathy for the Devil" by the Rolling … the Rolling Stones.'

I did not understand. I'd never owned that record. The only person I knew who had was Henri Fournier. Had he given it to Madame Desmaret, asking her to pass it on to me? One final gesture, a gift from another world, to let me know that, even if he couldn't see me any more, I had mattered to him? More drops of my reason spurted from my eyes.

'I see that you like "rock". That is what you call it?'

'Yeah. Although technically, that song actually has a samba rhythm.'

'Samba. And you are fond of the devil, Joseph, is that right?'

'Compassion,' I corrected him automatically.

'I beg your pardon?'

'In English, sympathy is "compassion". I mean, it can be used in the same way as *sympathie*, but for that song, I think it's about compassion.'

'I don't see what difference that makes.'

'It makes a big difference. I don't *like* the devil, I just feel compassion for him.'

'But why?'

'Because maybe it's not his fault. Maybe he wasn't born a devil, just a baby like all the others. Maybe he lost his parents, and he was sent to an orphanage, and that's where he became the devil.'

There was a long silence. I could hear nothing but the faint crackling of the bulbs in the corridor. The sliver of light under the door disappeared. In the distance, hinges creaked. That may, perhaps, have been the greatest satisfaction of my life: to have hit Father Sénac in the face through a locked door, to the rhythm of samba music.

There was no breakfast the next day. In fact, there were no more breakfasts for me in Oblivion at all; I had to make do with one meal each day. I was also no longer allowed to leave my cell to go to the toilet. Toad gave me a bucket instead, and one of the nuns came every day to empty it. Sénac stopped visiting me.

One morning, which I recognised from a vague greyish tinge to the darkness, I asked the nun how long I had been there. She must have pitied me because she looked around fearfully before whispering: 'Three weeks.'

Three weeks. Only three weeks of this eternity had passed, three weeks endured by the light of brief yellow flashes from the corridor. The door closed on my whirlwind thoughts, my indigo voyage, my astral drift.

Two or three days passed, according to my calculations, before I asked the same question to the same nun, who again looked around before answering in a murmur: 'Five weeks.' The priest came back on a night even denser than the others, a night like a vein of lignite.

'I know how you feel, Joseph. I know you hate me, just as I hated my teachers. But it is thanks to them that I am here today.'

'You're an orphan too, aren't you, Monsieur l'abbé?'

I had realised this somewhere between Jupiter and Saturn, on my way towards the frontiers of our galaxy. It had taken me a while. And yet I'd seen the sign, the one infallible sign. His hands shook.

'I told you before: there are no orphans, because we all have a Father. And that Father gave me a mission: to educate you. The world that awaits you outside is tough, and governed by rules. Each man must accept the place the Lord has assigned him. If we reject that place, what will happen? What will you say if your wife, one day, disobeys you? Or your children? You, too, will put your foot down. Listen to the words of Samuel: "But if you do not obey the Lord, and if you rebel against His commands, His hand will be against you, as it was against your ancestors." Do not force God to punish you as he punished your parents, Joseph. Think of the future.'

No, Monsieur l'abbé, I have seen the future. It is a better world, with flying cars and celestial switch points, men who transform into animals, maybe even into women, a world of frosted lemons and merciful volcanoes, a world of flags at half-mast because, thanks to Rose, flags will no longer have any meaning. A world where parents will not die, not so young. I have seen the future, and that is not the one you are offering me.

'Joseph, are you listening to me?'

'Christ didn't obey all the rules.'

'No, Christ did not obey all the rules. But he was Christ. And his coming had been heralded by prophets. Nobody heralded your coming, Joseph.'

'But if God made us in His image, we are Christ, every one of us.'

'A skilful sophism, dictated to you by your friend the devil. Put your intelligence to better use, in the service of faith. You'll be better off that way.'

The door at the top of the stairs slammed shut. The light went out. I retained it in my retinas, in yellow haloes that shrank until they became dots, and then nothing. I returned, without a struggle, to my solitude, to the penetrating silence of stopped clocks.

Eli, Eli, lama sabachthani?

One night, just before leaving me, as if it were some minor detail that he had just remembered, the priest whispered, almost inaudibly through the door:

'Your music teacher, the one you told me about ...'

'Monsieur Rothenberg?'

'That's it. He died.'

My first reaction was to laugh. Of course my old teacher wasn't dead! He had too many things to explain to me still. For instance, what he'd meant when he told me: 'Do not confuse rhythm and tempo, you stubborn fool. Rhythm is not a horizontal structure, it is vertical. It is dew that rises from the earth, what remains of a bell when it stops ringing. Do you understand?'

'No, Monsieur Rothenberg.'

'All the great Italian artists found rhythm, along with a handful of others whose names almost always begin with Van – Gogh, Eyck, Rijn, der Weyden. They found it and they hid it in their paintings. Now do you understand?'

I had things to tell him too. That I finally understood why he sounded so gloomy when he spoke the word 'lucky', when his eyes misted over and he muttered: 'I was lucky.' It was the same kind of luck I'd had when I was told I had to stay at home instead of boarding that aeroplane. And I wanted to tell him that I'd met a girl, a southern queen. That I wanted us to grow wrinkly together, like him and Mina.

'The elegance of the Czechs, the madness of the Russians, the humour of the Italians, the tragedy of the Germans, the arrogance of the French … that is what you need if you hope to become an acceptable pianist, my boy.'

'What about the English, Monsieur Rothenberg?'

'The English? If they applaud, you'll know you're an acceptable pianist.'

Rothenberg wasn't dead. He had to stay alive so he could call me a cretin, an idiot, an imbecile, because nobody did it as well as him.

'No, Monsieur l'abbé. There must be some mistake.'

'There's no mistake. He's dead.'

It had happened suddenly. Rothenberg had got up in the middle of the night and turned all the lights on in his apartment. When his wife had expressed her surprise at this, he had explained: 'I heard an extraordinary melody.' He had sat at his piano and had begun playing, very softly, while his wife went back to sleep. That was where she found him the next morning, a smile on his face, his hands on the keyboard. His beautiful, wrinkled hands still full of slaps to the back of the head that he would never distribute.

Wilhelmina Rothenberg had called Les Confins to pass on the news to me. She had offered to pay for me to travel back for my old teacher's funeral. Sénac had replied that I would unfortunately not be able to make it because I was bedridden.

'Let me go, Monsieur l'abbé. I swear I'll come back. I swear I won't say anything.'

'You won't say anything? About what?'

'Nothing, Monsieur l'abbé.'

'It's too late. The funeral was two weeks ago. You should be grateful that I concealed the true reason why you couldn't go. Besides, those people have some strange habits. They bury their dead so quickly that I don't know if you'd have got there in time.'

'Those people?'

'My word, the Jews.'

'You too?'

'What do you mean, me too?'

'If I was Jewish, would that be bad?'

'You're not, as far as I know.'

'No.'

'Then all is well. Very well, in fact. Good night, Joseph.'

My longest conversation with Sénac.

'I don't understand, Monsieur l'abbé.'

'What don't you understand, Joseph?'

'Why you do this.'

'And what did I do?'

'You protect Toad, for a start.'

'Monsieur Marthod ... I am the first to acknowledge that he is a difficult man. But one must understand him. He has seen things that would have broken the toughest men. His comrades falling in poisoned rivers. Why do you think he lives on the top floor, where no one can hear him? Is it you, Joseph, who gets up at night when he cries out? To cool his forehead, to purge the vicious venom that infects his sleep? So, yes, I protect him. I protect all of you. But let us forget Monsieur Marthod for a moment. What did *I* do?'

'You locked me up!'

'You're not locked up, Joseph.'

'So I can leave?'

'Of course you can leave. You have the key. That key is called humility.'

'You're a monster. A cold, loveless monster, incapable of tenderness.'

'I hardly remember my own father, but I do recall a tough man, a musician capable of playing the sweetest music after beating my mother, my brothers, my sisters. So forgive me if I do not believe in your tenderness, and forgive me also if I cannot bear the sound of piano music. You think I do not give you love? I give you God's love for his children. God's love is a love like diamond. It is colourless, it is cold. It cuts. I rebelled against it, when I was your age. I wanted to be a circus performer, a fire-eater, but my teachers did not let down their guard. I do the same for you, for your classmates. What my teachers taught me, I am teaching you. Because the world does not care about fire-eaters.'

'There must be another way ...'

'I don't think so, Joseph. That would mean that my teachers were wrong, and their teachers before them, and theirs before them.'

My longest conversation with the priest, and it never took place anywhere other than in my head.

That does not make it any less true.

This was the hard thing against which I ricocheted. Or perhaps I simply started to hear, because this whole story, right from the beginning, has been about ears. When I woke, I understood my greatest sin. It appeared, floating there in front of me, iridescent in the apocalyptic darkness.

The traitor had revealed the entirety of my plan. Toad and the priest could have stopped me as soon as I left the dormitory. They let me climb onto the roof, descend a rickety gutter, cling to icy cornices with my numb fingers, my limbs penetrated by long thorns of cold. I had insulted logic, statistics, gravity, all of them tetchy masters. They knew this and they let me do it, despite the fact that if I had fallen, someone at the DDASS would have opened an eye, yawned, perhaps decided to show some interest in what was happening at Les Confins. They submitted me to that ordeal of vertigo and ice because Sénac *believed* – with that ardent fervour of missionaries from another age – that it was for my own good. Sénac *believed* in the sinful nature of orphans, Jews, anyone who deviated from the certainties that another priest, another Toad, had forged in him with fists and fear. Monsters create monsters that create monsters. Sénac was vicious. Sénac was bad. But he was honestly vicious and bad. He was vicious and bad with the whole of his sick, cold heart.

When the priest returned that evening, I pressed my lips to the lock.

'I ask your forgiveness, Monsieur l'abbé.'

'Forgiveness for what, Joseph?'

'For forcing you to punish me. Because you are a good man. My punishment is also – above all – your punishment. You are suffering, more even than I, and that is my greatest sin.'

I held my breath.

The light went out, the door creaked.

The next morning, my cell opened to reveal Toad's yellow teeth.

'You've got class in an hour. You'd better not hang around in the shower too long. But don't skimp on the soap, because you stink.'

I was released after sixty-five days of isolation. If I look a little distant sometimes, forgive me. My eyes spent too long staring into oblivion.

There would be no jackpot. No chips tossed as tips to haughty croupiers. No strolls down Tropicana Avenue, between sand and tarmac, to go for a drink at the next bar, which, an hour later, would become the previous bar. There would be no convertibles, no shadowless palm trees against a backdrop of acidic nights. There would be no table just in front of the stage, there would be no stage at all. We would not go to Las Vegas.

Sinatra was the traitor. He had left Les Confins almost a month before I emerged, staggering and blinded, from my voyage underground, when I fainted almost as soon as I arrived in the classroom. I still had my winter eyes. Suddenly it was spring, a dazzling relief, pure blades of gold smashing against my temples. I was bedridden for a week, then I had to vacate the nurse's room for a little kid who couldn't stop vomiting.

Sinatra had been lying to us since the first time he was summoned by the priest. Frank had never sent any expert, never replied to a single one of his crazed letters. Sénac had told him, that day, that his biological father had made himself known and had begun the bureaucratic process necessary to release him from Les Confins. His father was a butcher from the Cahors region whose name was on Sinatra's birth certificate. There had been no tests to take, no doubts to which he could cling. Sinatra had stabbed himself in the arm with his compass to make it look like an injection. Because he was ashamed. Ashamed of that butcher from the Lot whom he had imagined a Vegas crooner. He had begged the priest not to say anything during the months of paperwork that would precede his release. Sénac had agreed, on the condition that Sinatra kept him informed about what was happening in the orphanage. 'And no peccadillos.' The priest only wanted something big, something serious. Sinatra had given him The Lookout.

With the patience of a spider, Sénac had let us continue, awaiting a graver, juicier sin: mine. Sinatra had wept as he admitted all this to Weasel, the day before his departure, when it had become impossible to keep the lie going any longer because everyone would see the short, bald, chubby man getting out of a van bearing the legend *Horsemeat, Fresh Enough to Neigh!*, everyone would see him as clearly as I see you now, stepping forward, awkwardly shaking Sinatra's hand, and ushering him into the passenger seat. Sinatra had left the way he had arrived, with his eyes lowered. I felt no pity for him. I swore that one day I would punch him in the face.

Our secret society no longer existed. The door leading to the roof had been sealed, Edison's radio confiscated, Marie-Ange confined to her valley. The members of The Lookout sagged under the weight of extra chores, driven to the edge of exhaustion. There was nobody up there any more, no watchers wind-bathing in astral storms to protect Les Confins, to keep a lookout over the planet. It was a year of massacres, of hijacked planes, of men killed for the colour of their skin – because only white was ever right – and it was the year the Beatles split up. Coincidences, perhaps. Rose had left the region soon after I was sent to Oblivion. We got the information from Étienne, who knew their gardener.

Toad had new orders: no communication was permitted between former members of The Lookout. At night, he would burst without warning into the dormitory to make sure that we were all in – or under – our beds. Weasel devoted himself to his bartering activities, Souzix fumed amid the little kids, Edison thought about the best way to go faster than the speed of light. Danny continued to stare into space and not talk to anyone. At least, since our last confrontation, he had given up picking fights with me. Only Momo was allowed to come near me – *Blessed are the poor in spirit* (Matthew 5:3) – because the poor are not dangerous. The priest chose another secretary, a fourteen-year-old blond boy who let the position go to his head.

I slowly returned to my half-life as an orphan. And finally became aware of secret glances, code signals, papers passed from hand to hand in a fraction of a second. One morning, Toad did not appear. The rumour went around that he had been taken to the hospital in Lourdes, where he had spent the night under observation. He had been accidentally electrocuted when he touched the light switch in the corridor by the entrance to his room. The phase cable had inadvertently become detached and had come into contact with the metal frame of the light switch. Toad had been thrown against the wall opposite by 220 volts of good Pyrenean electricity, which sometimes fluctuated – depending on dam releases – to as high as 250 volts. Enough to send your body flying one way and your soul another. Toad, having no soul, had survived. Edison looked strangely joyous all day long. Some orphans make very good electricians after all.

Weasel woke me at midnight, a finger to his lips. On the other side of the velvet curtain, where the little kids slept, what remained of The Lookout was waiting for me. Weasel slipped a bar of Poulain chocolate into a boy's hand, and the boy ran off to keep guard at the dormitory door, even if the absence of Toad – who was slowly discharging his batteries in a hospital bed – had greatly reduced the risk. A few sleepy heads looked up at us and Weasel hissed at them:

'Keep your little mouths shut if you don't want to wake up dead tomorrow.'

The heads immediately went back to sleep. The little kids' dormitory led to the shower room, and behind the worm-eaten door of the last cubicle we held our first meeting in three months.

'We are The Lookout,' announced Danny.

And we repeated it, filled with an odd emotion:

'*We are The Lookout.*'

'We're going to get out of here.'

'You're crazy. Wasn't the last time enough for you?' Weasel asked before looking at me. 'Not you too?'

'Do what you want. But I'm going. And so is Joseph.'

He had not asked my opinion. We were connected. We were brothers in darkness.

'Impossible,' Weasel said. 'The main gate is padlocked. And the priest had that part of the gutter near the fence removed. And even if we did get out, we couldn't escape through the cirque, and they'd catch us on the road.'

'We're not going through the cirque. Or on the road.'

'Oh yeah? So how do you plan to escape – fly?'

'The tunnel. Where the trains go. Nobody will bother looking for us in Spain.'

We were dumbstruck. Each one of us imagined the inside of that tunnel, the arched ceiling painted with the blood of all those poor souls who had had the same idea. Danny signalled to Edison, who unrolled a sheet covered with drawings and calculations, then began to speak.

'According to Étienne, the tunnel is five kilometres long. The trains go in every thirty minutes, in both directions. I've been timing them for two months, and the margin of error is about thirty seconds. That can mean thirty seconds more or thirty seconds *less*. Which means that, between two convoys, we have a maximum of twenty-nine minutes to reach the other end before another train enters the tunnel and smashes us to pieces. Let's say twenty-eight, just to be safe. We can go in after a train from France enters or after a train from Spain exits, but it makes no difference. Twenty-eight minutes.'

Edison spoke quickly, looking like an army general as he

moved his finger from sketch to sketch – stickmen, monstrous locomotives, crossed-out calculations, the sums done again and again to take into account every eventuality.

'For the sake of convenience, let's say that we wait for a train to enter the tunnel on the French side. We go in straight after the last carriage. The exit is five kilometres away. Rachid says an adult male, not an athlete but someone fit, can run an average of about ten kilometres per hour over a distance like that. So, if he hurried, he could get through the tunnel in twenty-eight minutes. The problem is that we don't have the muscular mass or the physical endurance of an adult. Which means that, to get through the tunnel before a train comes in the other way, we would have to be super-fit for our age. Questions?'

I raised my hand, which made the others smile.

'If a convoy takes four minutes to go through, why do they only send them through every thirty minutes? What if they decide to send them more often?'

'I asked Étienne that. It's a safety measure. One day, the Spanish pointsman went for a piss. When he came back, convinced that the train from France had passed, he sent in the next one. But the French train had broken down inside the tunnel and the driver was running to the exit to reach the emergency phone ... Carnage. It's an old, dangerous tunnel and there's no safety equipment. The thirty minutes are there to prevent another accident.'

Weasel shook his head.

'That's all well and good. But even supposing we don't end up painting a locomotive red, what are we going to do once we get to Spain?'

I knew that part of the plan, thanks to Rose.

'Nobody will look for us there. We'll be discreet, and we'll find jobs until we're old enough to do what we want. After that, we'll be free.'

'So who's coming?' Danny asked.

I raised my hand. Momo copied me. Weasel hesitated for a long time, then finally nodded. Souzix had had both arms raised all this time.

'Not you,' said Danny. 'You're too small.'

'I'm ten now! You're not going to leave me here, you bunch of bastards!'

'If you want to die … I don't give a shit. It's your choice.'

Edison knelt down next to him.

'Listen carefully. Danny's right. You can't run that fast. Even we're not sure of making it. What would be the point of you dying? And if you stay here, you'll become the leader of The Lookout. Your job is to recruit new members and make sure that our legend lives on. Can you do that?'

Souzix thought about this, chewing his lip in the gap between his teeth.

'Leader of The Lookout, huh …'

He puffed out his chest.

'Okay. But can I train with you anyway?'

'If you want.'

'We'll leave as soon as we're ready,' Danny concluded. 'One last thing: once you're in the tunnel, you can't stop running. Not for a second. You can't stop to get your breath back and you can't stop to help someone. There's no reason for two of us to die instead of one. Don't forget our motto.'

Our hands piled on top of one another. Our oath echoed under the damp, blue ceiling.

'*Every man for himself.*'

If Rachid was surprised when we asked him to help us train for a long-distance race, he didn't show it. Our PE classes, which had always been dreary hours spent hanging around doing nothing, were now transformed into moments of intense concentration, jaws tensed and cheeks pale, hours of dizzy spells and broadened shoulders and broken records. Momo, to everyone's surprise, was the best of us all. I don't know what dream he was pursuing when he ran, whether he saw the gloomy courtyard and its rusted fence or a golden beach in Algeria, a girl laughing as she ran ahead of him, where the sand was mauve. He was still sprinting when I was on my hands and knees, throwing up my breakfast. Danny ran inside his mind, absent from his own body. Weasel, Edison and I did our best. Souzix ran behind us, yelling: 'Wait for me! Wait for me!' We ran up the stairs, four steps at a time. At night, Danny woke us so we could do press-ups, lunges and squats. The orphanage succeeded where my callisthenics manual had failed. By July 1970, after several weeks of this, I could not recognise my reflection in the shower room's spotty mirror. I was metamorphosing into an athlete.

Despite our efforts, we plateaued at eight kilometres per hour over long distances. Only Momo flirted with eleven. At night, Danny insulted us. Weasel intensified his dealings, flooding the market with Poulain bars, and whoever was on kitchen chores would smuggle out second helpings. We ate dinner twice a day – in the refectory and in bed. Our exertions no longer made us vomit. Our muscles got used to the new workload and, pumped up by youth and strength, demanded more. Sometimes I would wake in the middle of the night, eager to exercise, and I would do pull-ups on the curtain rod that separated the big kids' dormitory from the little ones'.

Still we could not reach ten kilometres per hour. When we visited the mountain pasture, the members of The Lookout would run up the hill. Often we had to circle back to the main group so as not to arouse suspicion. Danny was the first of us to make the required speed. Spurred into action by our annoyance, we matched him soon afterwards. But that was only over shorter distances. Our calculations were based on extrapolations, and it was difficult to gauge our real capacity over the distance we would have to cross. Edison kept a secret diary of our progress, hidden in good company with the page from our encyclopaedia behind a pious image pinned to the wall of the dormitory: a bad-tempered Virgin that nobody ever touched and whose face, we had noticed from the detour he took to avoid passing close by it, frightened Toad. Edison estimated that we would need another two months of intensive training before we tried our luck. *Twelve kilometres per hour.* That was the speed we had to reach if we wanted to succeed.

'Sénac will get suspicious if we keep this up,' Weasel said miserably. 'I saw him watching us from his office window the other day when we were running.'

'Two months,' Edison repeated. 'Late September at the earliest.'

One morning in July – a year after Michael Collins had stared at the dark side of the moon while his friends, on the other side, were watching the earth rise – a commotion drew us to the courtyard.

Toad was waving Asinus about in one hand, shoving Momo away with the other. Momo was shouting, crying, reaching out desperately for his donkey. He was seventeen now, and his bum-fluff moustache had grown thicker. But Toad was strong and he kept him at a distance, his hand in the middle of Momo's face as if rubbing out a crude drawing.

'Aren't you ashamed? A kid your age with a cuddly toy? You know what they do to people like you outside? Anyway, this thing reeks. The best thing to do would be to throw it in the skip, don't you think?'

Momo howled and sobbed, but Toad, pitiless, continued to erase his face. Weasel and I exchanged a look. Danny shook his head.

'Every man for himself,' he muttered. 'We're not going to give up now we're so close. He'll just have to deal with it.'

Danny was right. In that exact place, at that exact time, he was right, and that was why we had to leave – to reach a country where he would be wrong. We were about to turn away when Rachid appeared out of nowhere, charged at Toad and smacked him in the head – a smack of breathtaking violence. Asinus went whirling through the air, his outstretched ears like wings, and dropped into Momo's arms. Toad swayed but did not collapse. He was in his fifties, he was fat, but he was as tough as a pioneer, as hard to kill as a scorpion. He charged at Rachid, who punched him in the gut. Toad bent double, red-faced with pain, but managed to trap Rachid's neck in a lock and wrestle him to the ground. Little kids started weeping, a nun screamed. Sénac emerged into the courtyard, alerted by the noise.

He advanced slowly towards the fight, taking off his cassock. The two men immediately jumped apart, shaking with mutual hate. Toad's eyebrow was cut and there was a crimson hand print on his cheek, a magnificent copy of cave art. Rachid had a nosebleed. They followed Sénac into the school.

Rachid was fired that day. He was not allowed to say goodbye to us. A kid who was on weeding duty saw him get in his car, and he swore our old PE teacher was crying. We never saw him again. Rachid doesn't know it, but we unanimously voted to make him an honorary member of The Lookout.

That night, only a few days before my seventeenth birthday, Danny woke us at midnight.

'It's time.'

The Spanish train had suddenly appeared, its petrol tanks swaying. A smell of grease followed in its wake, oppressive and sulphurous as vultures in flight. Nausea twisted my guts. Weasel was sweating so much, I could see him glisten in the night. Souzix had insisted on coming to see us off – he was ghost-white.

'It's too soon,' Edison said again, shaking his head. 'We're not ready. We need another two months. We won't make it.'

Danny climbed onto the ballast and scanned the night. A night of miracles, a cursed night.

'With Rachid gone, there won't be any PE classes for a while. There's no way we'd be able to train without Sénac getting suspicious. It's now or never.'

A faint metallic screech. Danny quickly moved out of the way. Sweat streamed down Weasel's face. I bent forward to puke, but nothing came. The clank and clatter of a dancing iron skeleton. Our train was coming, shaking its rusted bones.

'As soon as the last carriage has gone, run!' Edison told us. '*Between* the tracks, not on the sides – got it? There are lights on the tunnel walls – don't let them out of your sight. Give it everything you've got.'

Momo touched my shoulder. He was smiling, as usual, but shaking his head. Asinus's ears shook in sympathy. We were talking now without the aid of words, without their vulgarity and obviousness.

'You're not coming?'

He kept shaking his head.

'You never intended to come.'

Then he uttered the only two words I ever heard him say,

slightly deformed by lack of practice, forged in haste in the depths of his throat to ease our farewell.

'Better ... here ...'

We could feel the train's approach in our bodies, in the displacement of air that preceded it. *Better here*. Momo preferred Les Confins to the life that awaited us outside. I had been complaining about my status as an outcast, a pariah, since I got here. It took just those two words to make me understand that we were lucky. That there was something worse than being orphaned by one's parents: being orphaned by one's self. I took Momo in my arms and whispered in his ear: 'I'll come and get you.'

He pretended to believe it. The locomotive's headlights appeared, pushing a rectangle of light before them. A poet-engineer had named it A1A-A1A 68000. If I was going to be crushed by a train, I'd have preferred it to be by a *California Zephyr*, an *Empire Builder*, a *Capitol Limited*, or some other American locomotive with an epic name.

We turned to Souzix. He held out his hand, palm down.

'We are The Lookout.'

'*You* are The Lookout,' Danny corrected him.

The carriages rocked past, thundering into the vaulted black. The end of the train appeared, nibbled by the pursuing darkness.

'Get ready!' Edison yelled.

At the same moment, Étienne came out of his cabin, cigarette in mouth. The gardener stared at us in amazement. His eyes flicked from the train to the group of shivering orphans and he understood. The last carriage passed. Étienne opened his mouth, closed it again, turned on his heels and went back inside his cabin.

I couldn't run. It was impossible. I couldn't feel my legs any more.

'NOW!' screamed Edison.

He went first. Then Weasel, then Danny, and lastly me. Souzix, hand raised in farewell, slowly lowered his arm. And rushed after us, his ten-year-old legs carrying him as fast as they could.

I wanted to turn back. Danny's hand fell onto my shoulder, gripping a handful of flesh and fabric.

'He's already dead. And you've just lost ten seconds, you idiot.'

Every man for himself. I started to run again, to run like I'd never run before, to run away from Les Confins, to run away from the dead ten-year-old jogging behind us. Don't judge me. Every man for himself was not a selfish motto. It was a way of saying that, when nothing else mattered, *we* mattered. That we had value because, even if we were damaged, torn, we had a self worth preserving. The self that Momo didn't have any more, not really.

The faint glowing lights at the back of the train had vanished now. We followed the row of dim nightlights like a trail of breadcrumbs leading us to a distant, perhaps imaginary exit. The silhouettes of Edison and Weasel flickered ahead of me, tottering at the edges of absolute darkness. My lungs were burning. There was something familiar about this tunnel. Oblivion, of course. Oblivion and its expanded time. Impossible to know how long I had been running. Ten minutes. Two centuries. Someone was yelling and sobbing at the same time. My lungs. The sleepers beneath our feet, the crunch of the ballast, the stifling smell of creosote we were breathing. Slow down. I had set off too fast, I could not keep up this pace. A rookie mistake. Edison and Weasel had disappeared. Danny was somewhere behind me. Or ahead. My lungs again. I tried to catch my breath, to steal an atom of oxygen from this stingy blackness. My tongue like dough, my tongue that tasted of night.

Hours and hours running. Was there any point in praying? The prayer would bounce off the vaulted ceiling. *Even so, if there's someone up there, please help us. Amen.*

And then a sound, a metal lullaby. *No, not yet.* The tracks shuddered. On the other side, some sleepy guy had gone for a piss, had come back without bothering to wash his hands, had lit his pipe, warmed his fingers on the hot bowl, slowly pushed down on the switch lever. My mind rushed ahead of me, I saw the scene with hallucinatory clarity: the old man leaning on his damned lever, stubbly chin, cap askew, an image from the industrial age in a blizzard of phosphenes, in a racket of squeals and hums, of scorched breaths and singing metal. A puff of air on my face. Far ahead of me, something enormous had begun to move. A monster.

Another stride and I would give up. Another one. The silhouettes of Edison and Weasel reappeared against a background of stars. The exit. A two-ton horn roaring in the distance, the monster marking its territory. *Another three hundred metres. One stride equals one metre. Three hundred strides. But maybe one stride equals a metre and a half.* Ahead of me, the slice of night was growing wider. *Don't count.*

Run.

I emerged from the tunnel into the Milky Way, a Spanish night that in a single second enabled me to grasp flamenco, and *duende*, that word that few foreigners understand. I threw myself to the side and hurtled down a grassy slope, the only patch of green in red Aragon. Weasel and Edison were coughing up phlegm at the bottom of the slope. The train appeared, four hundred metres away, at the top of a hill. One single headlight: the face of a furious Cyclops. It was speeding up to reach the required eighty kilometres per hour. And Danny had not come out.

Two hundred metres.

He must have tripped.

One hundred metres.

And then I realised: Danny had entered the tunnel with no intention of ever coming out. Not in Spain, anyway. I waved my arms at the driver, shouted 'Stop, stop, stop!' But it was dark and we were at the foot of an embankment. The driver couldn't see us.

With the howl of a wild beast, Danny burst out of the tunnel, humpbacked, a fraction of a second before the train rushed in. He came running down the slope and his humpback fell off – it was Souzix. The two of them rolled to where I stood. The veins in Danny's forehead were throbbing blue-black, fit to burst. Lying in the grass, Souzix laughed. He laughed with his whole being. Danny stared up at a sky gold with stars and I thought for an instant that he was dead. Then I heard that strange sound, from the depths of his chest. He was laughing too. Danny was laughing.

The rhythm. That was when I heard it. It began with Danny's laughter. Danny who had run back to carry Souzix on his shoulders, a feat of urban legend, a feat like those of mothers who lift up the car under which their baby is trapped. Next, Rose's heart beating close to mine, a baby bird in Dior armour. And then the wind, and then the immense space between the notes, and then the joy of Souzix, who, for the first time in his life, was not surrounded by walls or fences. A joy that burst out in thick lines, some of which went astray and caused aeroplanes to explode; it was all connected, it was all there, within earshot.

The rhythm, the thing that held it all together, held our lives together. And I knew that, this time, I would not forget it.

I did not touch a single piano for the next two years. As Rose had predicted, I played again for the first time when I was eighteen in a dive bar whose owner hired me to 'add a bit of atmosphere'. I was hardly even rusty, and the bar fell silent. Those people were connoisseurs. It was the country of *cante jondo*, deep song, even if they had rarely heard it played so deeply. I played Aragon, the ochre stone of which its men and churches are built. I played that land of slow morning weddings where ploughs would sometimes bump over the bodies of murdered poets.

Souzix was caught six months later and sent back to France after being tied up in endless amounts of red tape. For Weasel, Danny, Edison and me, things were easier. We were young men with strong arms and, since we didn't expect much money, nobody worried about our age. We did piecework, constantly moving on, heading south, to distance ourselves from Les Confins.

We went our separate ways in Seville. At twenty-one I returned to France. I learned that Les Confins had been closed soon after our departure, officially because it was in a 'state of disrepair'. I never knew if it was because of our letter, if Rose had posted it, if our radiophonic idol had read it and alerted someone. I took possession of my inheritance. I had enough money for three lives. I became a piano teacher, choosing only students who interested me, in France and elsewhere. I will modestly admit that I was much sought-after. I have only one student today – I spend too much time outside. He's a promising kid, an irritating, talented idiot to the back of whose head I administer the occasional slap.

My money allows me to oil the right wheels. Momo did not appear surprised when I turned up one day at the children's home where he was employed, with a bunch of other self-orphans, recycling plastic bottle caps. I had promised to go back and find him and he had believed me. I installed him in the apartment next to mine, on the other side of the landing, and paid a carer to look after him. This is not generous of me. Momo saved my life, and I am still in his debt.

For all my efforts, I did not manage to find Rose. I didn't know her surname, Rue de Passy is a long street, and nobody seemed to know any counts there. And then, in 1984 – why that year, I have no idea – I heard the last thing I still had to hear. 'I'm not noble,' Rose had told me. Rose Leconte, daughter of Monsieur Leconte. I found a 1969 telephone directory: there had indeed been a couple named Leconte who lived at 46 Rue de Passy. I questioned all the inhabitants of the apartment building; nobody knew them. But the grocer, on the ground floor, did remember them – and little Rose, whom he had watched grow up. The family had left in the mid-1970s. Gone abroad, he thought. Rose had come to say goodbye to him. When I asked what her breathing had sounded like, he gave me a strange look.

It was during this period that I began to play every piano I could find, through open doors, through open windows, anywhere she might hear me. The fashion for public pianos opened up a field of infinite possibility. *If you played like that again, I'd recognise it right away, even if I heard you from the other side of the world.* I play *like that* now, the way I did at our first meeting, because I no longer play for myself. Having learned to listen to the world, I now play our story. My thousand-and-a-few-days-old sister, a Stones record in a suitcase, the hate of amphibians, the herbarium that must still be drying out there, in the shadow of the Pyrenees, the scent of lips that I barely touched, Rothenberg's speckled hands, motionless forever in Mina's speckled hands, the magma hiccups, the solar winds, I play Souzix running until he can't breathe, Danny stopping to die with him, I play life and death as if they were nothing, and they are nothing. I play the great white bulls, I play the evil and the joy that make up the air of our lives. My pianos in New York, Moscow, London, Valparaíso.

Rose became a diplomat, I'm sure. She travels and I swear that one day, on a gangway, getting off an aeroplane or a train, a weary ambassador, she will stop in her tracks, startled. She will come from Istanbul, Canberra, Vancouver. She will come from Tokyo or Tel Aviv. She will find me there, in front of her. She will recognise my voice. She will recognise the rhythm. I wait to feel her hand on my shoulder.

I will know it's her without turning around, without her having to say a word, because I am not deaf any more.

I hear everything.

Johann Sebastian Bach, orphan. Caravaggio, orphan. Ella Fitzgerald, Coco Chanel, orphans. Anton Bruckner, Louis Armstrong, Ray Charles, Billy the Kid, Tolstoy, Chaplin, orphans. And a thousand faces, at this very moment, a thousand faces that we do not know, not yet anyway, pressed to frosted windows, orphans.

I went to see Sinatra so I could punch him in the face. Edgar Calmet was his real name. This was the early 1980s, I think, an autumn day. It was raining on his village in the Lot, a mercury sky glowered down at the shop window of the horse butcher's, stuck between a bakery and a grocery that had closed years before. There was only one customer inside. I didn't recognise him at first through the misted glass. He had put on weight, his belly swelling beneath a long, meat-stained apron. He was balding and his eyes were sad. He looked up, caught my eye for a fraction of a second. I turned away without entering, without punching him in the face. I don't know if he recognised me.

Father Armand Sénac was awarded the Academic Palms and ended up in a retirement home for priests. I went to visit him, much later; my name meant nothing to him. He was feeding a sparrow, crumb by crumb, on his windowsill. His white hair dishevelled, his cheeks gaunt and covered by a tired, wispy beard, he wanted to know if I was the hairdresser he had been promised for a long time but who never came. I'm not sure he was the one I most blamed, this old son of nobody. The worst violence always has an excuse. The real culprits are those who had put him there, at the head of Les Confins, and will do so again. The guilty are the sons of somebody in their shiny shoes.

François Marthod, aka Toad, disappeared without trace after the closure of Les Confins. I feel no satisfaction at knowing he is dead – unless he is a hundred years old – but it does reassure me a little.

Jean-Michel Carpentier, aka Souzix, is now a projectionist at a cinema in the Hautes-Alpes, where there has not been a projector in a long time, or not like before anyway. Prior to the cinema, he was in prison. He doesn't like to talk about it, so we won't. I see Jean-Michel every year. I have to raise my voice – he is completely deaf in his right ear. None of his three marriages survived his desire to satisfy his encyclopaedic curiosity. Last year, for his sixtieth birthday, we went to see *Mary Poppins* together at his little cinema. He admitted having been angry with me for months when he realised that I had lied to him. It is possible he's still angry now.

Edison Diouf, our genius, returned to his village in the Jura and opened a small business repairing all kinds of electronic equipment. He had no equal when it came to aligning the tape heads of VHS video recorders, a technology, he claimed, that could easily have been improved, something he was happy to demonstrate with a soldering iron. He did not see the future, he did not see the silver polycarbonate discs that would succeed the cassette nor, even more incredibly, the 0s and 1s that unfurl inside wires of glass. Edison died in a hunting accident at the age of thirty-two. He was riding his bicycle in the forest, wearing a yellow jacket, an orange helmet and sunglasses. The hunter stated that he mistook him for a deer. A deer on a bicycle, in a yellow jacket and an orange helmet.

Antoine Loubet, aka Weasel, made his fortune in the import–export business. I never understood what it was he was importing or exporting. He lives in London and is even wealthier than me.

I visit him from time to time – the piano at St Pancras is one of my favourites. He is the only one of us to have had children, two beautiful girls. He became a grandfather recently. Antoine is not well: his lungs are full of the apartment building that collapsed on his childhood and left his street like a toothless smile, his bronchial tubes filled with that absence that will soon take his life, and then we will be able to say that the building killed all its inhabitants.

Daniel Minotti, aka Danny, has been constantly on the move ever since we escaped. He roams the planet, sets down his bag, does some work or lives on what people give him, then sets off again. Occasionally he washes up on my doorstep. He swears that his vagabond days are over, that he can't do it any more, that this time he will settle down for good. Sometimes he starts crying, for no apparent reason, especially if we've been drinking. He whispers: 'You know ...' but never finishes his sentence. Early in the morning, I hear the door creak. Danny leaving again. One day, he won't return.

Maurice Noguès, my old friend Momo, still lives next door to me. His carer has moved in permanently. The wise age more quickly and, in his eyes, night is already falling on his azure childhood. He no longer has epileptic fits, but he finds it hard to get around, his long body folded up in a velvet armchair, a pile of grey cloth that used to be a donkey in his lap.

It is getting late, Madame, Monsieur. My story is nearing its end. One last thing.

Go and see Momo, please. Go and see Momo before it's too late. You can ask him if what the old man told you – the old man who plays the piano in train stations, airports, in all those different transport hubs – is true. He will nod his head and he will smile.

The last train has just arrived, the 00:35 from Barcelona. She isn't on it. The cafés are closing, the shutters are coming down. It is a peaceful, orphan hour. It is time for us to part.

I have an early start tomorrow.

To Gérard P.
and to all those who were not able to escape.

The author would like to thank:
Daniel Glet for generously drawing
the opening bars of Beethoven's opus 27, no. 2.;
the Centre National du Livre for its support in the writing of
this novel;
Laurent Perez del Mar for his friendship, his music,
and 'Les Adieux' played over the telephone;